As My World Falls Down

– A Queen of Blood and Glitter novella –

Benjamin Kissell

For my – *for our* – fans:
Thank you.
For my family – blood and chosen:
I love you.

Bibliography:

Humor (anthologies)

Retail Hell: Little Monsters – 'Sticky Fingers' (2012)

Retail Hell: Discount Hell – 'Maryland Brown'n'Dirty' (2012)

Retail Hell: Stolen Hell – 'Stability is Highly Overrated' (2012)

Retail Hell: Coworker Hell – 'The Devil Wears Walmart' (2012)

Fantasy (anthologies)

America in Twilight – 'A'Sleeping Beauty', 'WinnebaGODS on High' (2015)

Shadows Within the Labyrinth – 'A Case of Moon-Cold Silver' (2017)

Cocky Tales – 'Cocky King Neckbeard' (2018)

Rejected – 'Soft as Snow, White as Moon' (2020)

Beyond Calliope's Garden – 'Heartsease' (2020)

A Queen of Blood and Glitter series:

'A Queen of Blood and Glitter' – 2019

'Between the Forest and the Stars' – 2020

'As My World Falls Down' – 2021

'A Throne of Ill-Made Will' - forthcoming

TABLE of CONTENTS

PREVIOUSLY

in

A QUEEN OF BLOOD AND GLITTER

Faeries are real.

In 1871, in several spots throughout the world, the veils between the hidden realm of Faerie and the world of man thinned to the point of breaking. The most notable was in an area along Hedgeman's River in Carterburg, VA – an historic town halfway between Richmond and Washington DC.

There, along the river, the Fae began to build a life for themselves; one where joy mingled with trouble as the two races struggled for balance.

In the shadows of the city's burgeoning Fae District, a young faerie suffered the greatest loss; his heart was riven at the murder of his one-true-love.

In its wake, he was glitteringly reborn as the moon-cold silver Blodeuwedd. Now, almost 150 years later, Blodeuwedd lives and thrives as the popular and enigmatic drag queen, Miss Nomer; a faerie with secrets, bitter truths, and a want for vengeance.

He entrances his fellow queer and Fae within the confines of *The Crossroads*, the bar at the center of Fae life, as he dances along the knife's edge between nemesis and protector.

Circe, yes *that* Circe, is a shapeshifting Sidhe Cat who would prefer quiet nights drinking coffee and munching chocolate biscuits in the lovely confines of The Hollow Hill; a lifetime of struggles forgotten.

Unfortunately for her peace of mind, as an insatiably curious Faerie and cousin to the High Queene of Faerie and the Selighe Court, HRH Mabh Grainne, she has been charged with investigating any and all mysteries that impact the state of affairs between Man and Fae.

The last few years have seen Tamlinn, her best friend, joining her as they root out the threads that bind the threats of The Phosphorescent – a gay gang of swordfighting Fae – and the Unselighe Court and its dark Queene Angroboda, with the troubles and deaths plaguing Carterburg.

As adventures and mysteries tugged, Circe and Tamlinn kept finding themselves pulled back to *The Crossroads* and its enigmatic proprietrix. Whether for good or ill, their lives became entwined; especially when Tamlinn met the charming Simon, whose life was Faerie-touched years before by Miss Nomer's own actions.

The point of no return arrived when the Unselighe Queene delivered an ultimatum to Blodeuwedd and his friends – Johann The Lady Ophelia, DJ Nomios Phuc, and The Material Girls: Either join Her against the Selighe Court or declare themselves Her enemy and prepare for all of the death and misery that would entail. Faced with these two choices, Blodeuwedd saw no other route and took up his crown as the Queen of Blood and Glitter. Before the next Hunter's Moon, he plans to center his new Court between Carterburg and his mother, the fearsome Queene Angroboda.

Will Blodeuwedd's actions, his desire for vengeance, blind him and damn those he's come to care about or can he save himself and all those who've come to care for him before The Hunter's Moon when Angroboda and the full array of the Unselighe Court make their move?

Only the next few months will tell ...

1

"Bitch, you have >got< to be shitting me," the faerie muttered.

Looking up, a comely shape of midnight shadows and starry nights worked her magic on the central stage. Clad in an intoxicating mish-mash of Baroque finery, fishnets, and a black leather jacket covered in AB stones, she held the throngs of club-goers in the palm of her well-manicured hand. With them in her thrall, the unparalleled proprietrix of *The Crossroads* herself – the ever-confounding Miss Nomer – danced.

"Well, damn."

Her mountainous black wigs – threaded with luminescent pearls, shards of amethyst, onyx and jet and pinned with two star-bright combs – and spiraling silvery horns asynchronously pirouetted about the stage; while her lithe, angular frame – inhuman in its perfection – rippled and vibrated to the beat.

Impossibly-high heels, their crocal purples kissed by inky gems and silvery glitter, hovered above the lacquered wood of the stage as she swung, gyrated, and contorted in sparkling midair – not a wire to be seen.

Held solely in her magic.

Her face, knife-sharp and pale as a newborn moon, shone beautiful amidst the Glamoured blacks and shadowy violets she'd garbed herself in. Upon her pointed cheeks the petal-marked gemstones and black pearls shimmered in sympathy.

With an elegant flick of the wrist her hair became unfettered; falling down in idealistic tumbles of living curls. Their inky blackness studded with violet and indigo starscapes that spread out across the revelers like living, undulating clouds of starry magic.

The two combs, crescent moons in silver and diamond, caught and reflected the club's electric and faerie-blessed lights; mesmerizing all and sundry in their brilliance.

The space was thronged with young mortal and Fae revelers – laughing, dancing, drinking, and flirting – and the activity was mirrored above as, beyond the audience's heads, the ceiling was alive with activity. Streamers of rainbow'd light danced to the heavy bass (glittering as they fell upwards and sideways – never down) while half-clad (or less) in silver- and gold-lamé Go-Go boys and girls twirled on Glamoured trapeze wires of light and glitter.

Amidst the colorful chaos – as Glamours danced ever outwards across the dance floor – a thick, vocoder'd voice, heavy with vocal fry, sang; urging them to dance until the world ends.

"Britnexcuze me?"

Tamlinn – errant Elf Knight and agent of the Queene – turned and found himself chest to padded-bosom with Helena Bottom Parter.

While *The Crossroads* resident drag troupe, The Material Girls, had a large rotating cast of regulars and guest performers, he'd recognize this queen anywhere.

Her chartreuse and aqua hair, a riot of perfectly-styled braids and locs, shone in stark contrast to the Black queen's dark, gleaming skin; a nude-illusion dress, slinky and dripping in dangling crystals of emerald and azure, somehow left little and oh-so-much to the imagination as he stared at her.

"My eyes? Are down here," Helena Bottom Parter joked, bouncing the breastplate by hand with enthusiasm and a gleam to her oak-brown eyes. Batting her pale pink 301 lashes, she cocked her head and leaned in closer, a smile on her voice, "It's been too *long*, Tamlinn, since I had the *pleasure* of your company."

A flush suffused his cheeks, as the layered hints and innuendos of the queen's comment washed over him – few had ever managed to achieve that perfect balance of ribald flirt and humor; most tended to heave him feeling uncomfortable, instead of flattered – before his general demeanor of affected-stoicism and wry wit regained its footing.

Waggling his own brow, he seized Helena's hand and dipped low – his tousled dark hair and twining horns grazing the jewels that danced at her thigh as he bowed.

"My apologies, mamselle," he answered, regaining his full height. "I shall do my best to *rectify* that in the near future – although," he dropped his blue eyes in exaggerated innocence and leaned closer. "I fear that our respective boyfriends might take umbrage, were we not careful in our meanings."

Helena laughed, a clear and infectious note from somewhere beneath bodice and padding, as she wrapped her elegant arm about his and led him back towards the DJ booth.

"Never fear – nor should your young man – Sigmund?" she teased.

"Simon," he corrected, smiling.

"Simon has nothing to worry about, nor does Danny," she jutted her chin upwards towards a young man hanging above them. One of the club's more talented (and popular) Go-Go boys, Danny was tall – nearly seven foot – and svelte; showing off his lean frame and bright-blue tattooed Black skin (its velvety sheen showed off his Selkie parentage) in the club's ubiquitous costuming, he grinned down at them. Danny's natural, genial tones overrode the glam stage persona of Helena's sex-star and often revealed the sweet boy beneath the wig.

Danny swam a figure eight in midair as Tamlinn and Helena looked on, "He's done his damnedest at making an honest man out of me and I think it took." She smiled, an intimate warmth reserved for friends and family, suffusing his face beneath the Glamours and the make-up.

"Well! My congratulations to you both."

"Many thanks, Sir Knight. Blo's throwing an engagement party for us next week – he's even threatened to close the whole of *The Crossroads* to allow us privacy." She paused as a pair of Brownies skirted past, trays laden with drink, beneath the tall, ornate stand and stairs that led to the club's private DJ booth.

Within its confines, Nomios Phuc – his attention lost to the music – spun the beats and, from a pair of glowing consoles at either hand, controlled the club's main Glamours with two slight Fae to aid him. As Tamlinn looked to the right, passing into the hallways for staff and queen, he saw Marlena tucking bills into a handbag Glamoured like a great, gleaming spring green boa; her honey-blonde, dark-rooted wig and barely-there skirt shiny with sweat and glitter.

"It's 'Much Ado About Britney' night, where each queen does a Britney Spears song or performance mash-up," she answered his raised brow. "Bonus points if you tie in a Shakespeare reference into one of your numbers. You already missed my 'Lucky'/ 'Lucky Star' mash-up as Ariel from 'The Tempest' – yes, before you ask, I'll forgive you – and Ophelia's '(I Got That) Boom Boom' take as Lady MacBeth was EPIC, to be honest. That bitch can moooooove better than any of the twinky windmilling-queens and is so fucking creative." A look of glee lit up Helena's eyes as she remembered.

"Oh, and Faun de Ling and Ky Li'aison did an amazeballs version of 'Scream and Shout' – with actual flaming disco balls – well, they were Glamoured, but still! If you stick around, Ophelia opens after the intermission with a 'Circus' / 'The Greatest Show' mash-up and then it's my second number, an 'If U Seek Amy' remix with – well, you'll have to see," Helena's enthusiasm was contagious.

"Depending on how long this meeting is, Simon and I have a date afterwards where we plan to hang out for nibbles in his favorite booth and dancing on that light-up floor 'til the wee hours – he's due in," Tamlinn smiled as he pulled out his phone to check the time. "Shit, less than hour!"

Seeing the suddenly-empty stage and DJ-less booth, neither Phuc nor Nomer anywhere to be seen, Tamlinn kissed Helena's cheek just aside the Glamours and turned towards the same hallway Marlena had disappeared down. "Expect me when you see me," he called over his shoulder.

The queen smiled as he ran, "I hate it when he goes, but, I certainly love to watch him leave," she muttered to herself before returning to the throng of revelers and heavy-tippers.

Threading his way past various bar-backs and staff, he turned towards the hallway branching off into the adjacent building – converted into the club's expanded storage, dressing rooms, and (of course) into Miss Nomer's private offices.

Knocking thrice on the rowan and oak door, he was greeted by Circe and Nomer – the delicious smell of hickory-smoked fire, coffee and biscuit wafted throughout the well-appointed rooms.

"Finally – I was starting to wonder if you'd gotten lost," Circe greeted him with warmth and snark as she passed him his own china cup and saucer as he sat, the supple leather of the armchair squeaking as he made himself comfortable. Nomios Phuc, already ensconced with tea and a large cucumber sandwich, sat in the adjacent chair and smiled – pinky up.

"This is Nomer's special, private brew and bluddy delicious," she added, dunking a chocolate-and-hazelnut biscuit into the steaming cup.

"Thank you, Enchantress," Nomer smiled from behind the desk, tight but genuinely as she half-closed her eyes, dipping her forehead slightly forward. Her hair was already back up into its usual ebony mountain of coils and curls.

Behind them, all along the door and its wall, faint sigils in glittering black, smoky violet, and shimmering silver danced – resealing the room's wards. Resting her hand against a large teak box, she opened her eyes again – their startling silverness always managed to catch Tamlinn off-guard.

"To what do I owe this visit – as I doubt it merely a social call, delightful as that would be."

"Were it so, we both would have a far kinder time," Circe sighed, her golden-ginger riot of hair shining in the room's firelight, as she set the cup and saucer on an empty side table at hand. "Sadly, trouble is come to both our doorsteps."

2

FLASHBACK – five nights ago

No matter how many late nights he pulled in the museum – and the last year had seen many of them, Ciaran always felt uneasy in the records room when the sun went down. It wasn't the shadows – the Carterburg Museum was filled with them; shadows rustling in corners and high-arched ceilings – and it wasn't the occasional moan the rafters let out as the wind whipped and wound about the venerable, old downtown building.

No.

It was the way the eyes of the tall portraits that lined the southern wall would follow you – whether by lamplight or candlelight, the eyes of Carterburg's elite and moneyed watched the goings on. Gilt frames and oiled canvases filled the wall with faces of old and moneyed men and women who looked down their noses – quite literally by the placement of the card catalogues, filing cabinets, and map drawers directly beneath them – at the researchers and librarians who toiled away.

Ciaran was a self-possessed little man, balding but with a handsome mien and an air of quiet dignity; he dressed in tweeds and twills with sharply-cut trousers and, although his coat was getting quite threadbare at the elbows – he kept meaning to ask Pernilla about how to fix that, he would arrive at work each morning with a smile and his customary beaker of dandelion-and-acorn tea.

Ciaran, a working nickname he'd long grown to prefer to his native born Chios Rann, was a Lares – a type of household faerie often assumed to be 'the ancestors' who watched over and aided the family. He'd served Her Royal Highness, Queene Mabh, since the days of Delphi – helping to prune and manage the 'truths' and breadth of knowledge mortal books and libraries held on the Good Neighbors. It was a matter of state record – sealed from human eyes of course – that during the Alexandria fires, when the great library was aflame, he rescued no less than 400 rare scrolls of Faerie/mortal history. Those selfsame scrolls were safely ensconced in the Royal Library of Koîloros – the private, royal residences within The Hollow Hill.

He stood no taller than a child (his forehead was even with the plane of his desk in the cubby beneath the winding stairs). His ears jutted up and to the side in a rather becoming manner, neither threatening to human eye nor terribly comical, with straw colored eyes and a quick smile to coworker and the occasional visitor to his unassuming corner of the museum alike; he liked his job and, in turn, was liked for it.

Tonight, as he tapped the banker's lamp at his elbow to increase its glow, he felt a growing unease that had nothing to do with the chill late-January airs.

The austere faces of Lady Gresham, Betty and Fielding Washington Lewis, Lord Ravensclere, (the first and only) Lord and Lady Stuart, and the dozen other gentlefolk which flanked the hall all seemed most severe in their looks; their eyes boring down at him in cold judgment of the compiled accounts and paperwork now in his hands.

The Stuarts.

The family line was one of Carterburg's oldest and (for a long time) most respected – exceeded only by the Carters themselves and the town's most famous family, the Washingtons – with records tracing it to Scots emigrants in the late 17th century (when Carterburg was merely a port for loggers, explorers, and merchantmen). He'd found that during the late 18th century land and commercial deeds showed their rise in status due to savvy business deals and canny (if not opportune) marriages. It surprised him, although he couldn't say why, that the Washington Lewises had co-signed the deeds and contracts to the two block stretch along the river northeast of Williams Wynd. That selfsame stretch where burgeoning tenements, taverns, and town homes swiftly sprung up as Carterburg grew in trading import – before they were, eventually, bought out by the Stuarts in a (presumably) amicable agreement.

The deeds to several of the tin and gold mines in the area showed their names as primary shareholders (the family had even deeded the city Alum Springs Park after the minerals had dwindled in the 1850's – preceding the arrival of Faeries and the death of industrial construction in the area).

For a time in the 19th century, the area's premiere vineyard was the Stag's Eye, owned by Robby Stuart. All of the names and titles, deeds and accounts hinted at a prosperous family – and yet, by the early 1870's, in the aftermath of the American Civil War and the arrival of the Fae, the family had only a few living members left. Their dynasty had now dwindled to a grandmother, mother, her husband and two daughters, and – by marriage – several distant cousins.

They'd had six children; three sons (two died in the Battle of Carterburg and the third of sealed-by-gubenatorial-edict circumstances in 1874) and three daughters – the eldest died, childless, of cholera in 1871. It was the youngest, Lucy (whose portrait with her husband, Alistaire, seemed to glower down at Ciaran), who'd entered service to the Queene of Faerie in hopes of improving the family's estates (was the rumor at the time) and emerged as the first – and only – Lady

Stuart. While the family had property remaining, Lucy saw the family's wealth dwindle further and further – despite constant rumors of hidden faerie gold – until their home, *On a Whim*, was the family's sole estate.

The Carters, he'd noted, had been one of the biggest beneficiaries of their slow decline – buying more than half of their properties and holdings over a fifty year period.

Her sister married, but had no children of her own, and Lucy bore only one child who, in turn, only had one child, and she had but one daughter as well – the recently murdered Marleigh Lyn Stuart-Miller.

Ciaran winced, recalling the easy and good-natured laugh of Marleigh Lyn when she'd visit him and the records department; coffee and a homemade scone in-hand. Despite the shadowy hints his search produced, that even she bore her own crimes – he missed her. Now, with her gone, all that remained of the vast Stuart family were some distant, impoverished cousins and a pocket of the Millers (some of whom had married into the Carters in the 1980's). The house and land Lady Lucy Stuart had gained from Queene Mabh had returned to Faerie hands, held and run by the Brownies and Hobs who'd lived on the property for the last century.

The things he'd learned in the darkest, deepest half-worded notes, personal ledgers and diaries left an acrid taste in his mouth. He'd read endless pages of blackmailed business, underhanded mercantile works, stolen jewels, double-dealings during war, and extortion from tenants and business 'partners' alike going back generations.

The way the lamplight caught her just now, as he looked up at her portrait, it almost looked like Lucy Stuart could shed a tear.

Her mother and father had tithed Lucy to the Queene of Faerie in hopes of regaining their lost foothold in society (and the rumors of endless faerie gold didn't hurt their hopes, either). They'd also threatened to evict her grandmother, whose health was failing, from the grand brownstone without a penny if Lucy didn't comply. For a planned seven years she – and two other young women from Stefford and Spotswood – served the Faerie Queene in Her private and public quarters. He remembered Lucy from those days; kindly, nervous, and incredibly shy. What struck him most, just then, was that before her service was done, and the contract concluded, she left rather unwillingly; crying and trying not to make a scene, but making one regardless as she blubbered, her lustrous red hair almost lank.

Perhaps, he mused, glancing up at Lady Lucy's somber face, that was why the Queene had been so generous in Her gifting and specific in its stipulations – that her descendents would have the granting, but Lucy's parents did not receive one penny directly from the Queene.

The painting showed a quiet young woman in her thirties, poised but vulnerable; her attire was a lovely violet-touched grey and high-worn in the Victorian style, while her coppery hair was pulled into a large bun with artfully-teased coiled over her shoulder, and a great gem, set amidst a sea of starry blue stones, sat on her bosom.

An odd sound pulled the Lares' attention away from the painting; standing in a rush, he knocked over the top of the haphazard stack of papers and notebooks beside him.

A great shadow seemed to pull itself from the furthest corner, congealing.

Dry, sandy heat seemed to permeate the room as the shadow stepped forward; crackling and creasing old parchment as it went.

Ciaran, his nerves frayed and tingling, dropped from his seat and stared, leaning against the great leg of the table – too frightened to make more than light whimpers against this.

Emerging from the inky shape was a Faerie woman.

Tall she was and barefoot; her skin was sun-darkened like an ancient brazier and pulled tightly over her bones. Her garb was simple, ash-white linen kissed by countless dark flames about its edges; a simple collar of burnished gold and lapis beads clung to her bare breast. About her, clinging to the gloom, her hair was as dark as a moonless night and silky straight. As she emerged from the liquid shadows her face shone like bone – no, Ciaran realized, it was bone. A naked jackal's skull wreathed in a halo of unlight beneath a dancing flame of phosphorescent green, while two raven's wings, oil slick black, danced where her ears might have been. All about her the scent of burning bronze and old, old blood dried on stone.

Unselighe!

From either side, two Menacing Hobs – their skeletal frames and elongated craniums corpse-pale in the wan light – emerged to flank the jackal-headed woman. Their grins, all knife-sharp teeth and lipless menace, faintly glowed in the thin light.

Frightened more than he could ever recall, Ciaran turned on his heel to run.

Reaching for the stack – for his Queene's work – he found himself slipping on a loose sheet of paper that must have fallen when he bolted from his seat. His forehead collided with the edge of the oaken foot – carved, he noted somewhere in the back of his mind, in the shape of a griffin's forepaw.

As he passed out, the warm darkness taking him, he just made out the slippery shape of the woman clawing the painting of poor Lucy Stuart.

3

Official Court Investigator Case File (Supplemental) - February 3rd

Taliesin dropped by last night while Tam and I were having dinner – our usual 'when not out sleuthing' Tuesday night affair of sushi, wine, and vintage Hollywood films (I still can't believe Tam's never seen 'Bringing Up Baby') – and "requested" our aid on a case.

One that was "near to the Queene's heart" and on the extreme q.t.

With a grim look, he handed me a small folder and left.

After reading his sparse notes – seriously, the man is a Bard for the Norns' sake, you'd think he'd be able to expound at least a bit in a sensitive report; but no-oh – we eschewed the film (dammit) and turned in for the night, deciding to start our investigation bright and early this morning.

Something tells me, after where this morning has led us – across Carterburg's well-heeled residences, venerable museum, and back again – that this is the type of case that always leaves me with wrinkled whiskers and wasps stinging at my thoughts.

Oh goodie goodie gumdrop.

END FILE

. . . .

As always, the tableau that greets me upon my entrance to *The Crossroads* is different in a dozen little ways.

While the coat check room and Bouncer's station remain in their constant spots, the carpet in this section of rooms is a deep hazel tonight – it'd been a lovely heather violet last week, and while the wood that encircles the far wall is still a light pine the seats' upholstery are suddenly the color of a stormy sea at dawn; the mirrors behind the bar have a golden 'mercury' look to them tonight and the candles and Will-o'-the-Wisps which dance about are iridescent shades of sea foam and ocean depths.

Thankfully, the inviting smell of the large coffee machine is the same.

Sidling up to the bar, I look for my favorite bartender – the dryad Orielle is easy enough to spy, her height and manner alone make her stand out (the grey-green bark skin is also a dead giveaway) – and wave her over.

"Evening, Orielle – is Miss Nomer in tonight?"

"She is – although she's about to go on – you can probably catch her near her offices if you rush."

"Thanks," I smile and then decide, turning back before leaving. "Would I be able to have some of that wonderful, 'Boss Only, private brew' coffee?"

She laughs and I'm suddenly back on Aeaea – the roar of the sea and the soft kisses of sunlight through myrtle and pine as nymphs and Nekks dance about me.

"She said that you had free access to it – I'll have one of the Hobs bring some by her office here in a few."

Sweet Charites, that? Is a blessing in and of itself.

Wending my way towards the far-back corridors reserved for staff and performers, I make my way to the sturdy door that marks Blodeuwedd the Miss Nomer's private offices. Before I've even rapped on the smooth surface, the door swings open and I see the queen – literally, since she's been crowned the Queen of Blood and Glitter – as she adjusts her costume before a Glamoured mirror; made from rippling water, it shines with frosty moonlight about its edges.

"Welcome Enchantress – come in."

While I may adopt this feminine shape that I was born into when needs-be, preferring the sleek and ginger furred form of a Sidhe Cat, the femininity and *otherness* that Blodeuwedd employs is miles beyond me. The art of drag – let alone the magicked and Glamoured drag of Nomer and company – is one that he employs as her to such an impeccable degree that I'm momentarily gobsmacked as I watch her smooth hair, tuck fabric, and adjust pins.

"I'm sorry that I've but a moment before I'm due on stage – please sit; it's not a long number, maybe six or seven minutes and I'll return as swift as I can."

"Thank you," I smile as I drop into one of the lovely leather armchairs in a semicircle before the great desk. "If I may, when you return – would you bring Phuc with you?"

Her brow manages to arch even higher – which is astonishing, considering the brow is painted almost beside her hairline – before she nods, a ghost of a smile beneath the lip tar and Glamour, and exits the room in sparks of jet and silver; the mirror disappearing in smoke and glitter behind me.

I haven't done more than pull out my tablet, the case files already opened, before Orielle appears in the doorway with a tray of china cups and saucers, delicious chocolate-and-hazelnut biscuits, a small pot with tea, and the heavenly aroma of coffee.

"Thought I'd deliver in person, but, sadly, I can't stay and chat, Chat," for some reason she's taken to calling me 'cat' in French. It's weird, but cool. I think I actually like it. "There's a thirsty hen party – buncha bridesmaids and a bridezilla – in the private rooms and my 'expertise' at calming them down is needed."

She disappears in a breeze of leafy hair and mossy perfume and I am suddenly left on my own to wait for the return of the club's proprietrix.

Thankfully, there's coffee.

·········

"Sorry about that, Enchantress," Miss Nomer saunters into the room, her hands buried in the mass of black wigs atop her head, pinning the 'do back up into a semblance of order; which leaves me wondering just what in the nine realms she did to unsettle that mass of wigs and pins. Behind her, a tray of cucumber sandwiches in-hand, is Nomios Phuc.

"Nothing to apologize for – after all, I'm the one showing up unannounced," I smile as she sits behind her desk – delicately taking the china and pouring herself a steaming cup of coffee. Each time the carafe releases its steam, a new wave of the heady aroma washes over the room – it's nigh intoxicating.

"Sandwich, Blo?"

"You know, I just might," her tone is warm (for her) and indulgent as she takes one of the proffered nibbles from Phuc as he sits.

From what I've gathered, I could count on one paw the number of folk who've seen the lithe queen eat more than sparingly – and that includes the dinner last winter at Ravensclere Manor where she mostly pushed food about her plate after biting two buttery asparagus tips.

She must catch sight of my own quirked brow as she smiles, mid-bite, and swallows (no lipstick smudge on her teeth), before dryly laughing.

"I don't often eat in drag – it lowers your street value."

I can't help but snort at this sage advice, nearly spilling my precious coffee; unsure if it's the sentiment or merely her delivery that I find it so damned funny.

"Dance. Magic. Dance. Refuel," she smiles ruefully as she rubs the back of her neck with one hand, the last bite of sandwich in the other. "On show nights, it feels as if that's all I do; as I'm sure you're familiar, trying to keep up one's energy whilst expending so much in Glamour is …" she waves her black-lacquered and beglittered nails about as she swallows the last bite.

"No mean feat," I finish for her.

"In fact – would you pass me one of those delightful biscuits?"

"They're a special recipe," Phuc smiles around a mouthful of cucumber sandwich, pulling the tray across the desk towards her before turning back to me. "Wendy – a highland Brownie of considerable skill and our Head Baker – has been baking them since the 17th century, believe it or not. She swears," at this, Phuc lowers her voice to a stage whisper, "that apple-and-acorn flour, instead of wheat, is the secret to their lightness."

I file this tidbit away, in the back of my mind under 'delicious treats to suggest to Lavender for my next visit to *On a Whim*' – she's still made the best coffee I've tasted outside of Nomer's private blend in centuries. And am about to comment when, after a light treble knock, the door swings open to admit Tam – looking both handsome and harrowed as he saunters in.

"Finally – I was starting to wonder if you'd gotten lost," I smile and pass him a cup and saucer as he sits, the supple leather of the armchair squeaking as he shifts his lanky frame.

"This is Nomer's special, private brew and bluddy delicious," I incline my head in our hostess' direction, dunking a chocolate-and-hazelnut biscuit into the steaming cup as I do so.

"Thank you, Enchantress," Nomer smiles from behind the desk, tight but genuinely as she half-closes her eyes, dipping her forehead slightly forward.

I sense less than see that, behind us, all along the door and its wall, faint sigils in glittering black, smoky violet, and shimmering silver dance – resealing the room's wards. When she's finished, she leans against the desk ever so slightly, resting her hands against a large teak box before, finally, opening her eyes to resume our conversation.

"To what do I owe this visit – as I doubt it merely a social call, delightful as that would be."

"Were it so, we both would have a far kinder time," I sigh as I set the cup and saucer on an empty side table at hand. "Sadly, trouble is come to both our doorsteps."

No one in the room is shocked by my pronouncement, Nomer least of all.

"Five nights ago," I begin, "the Carterburg Area Cultural History Museum was broken into – by magickal means – and a Lares of Royal Employ, working within the confines of the Museum and the city's records' offices was attacked; his confidential papers were stolen and he's been unconscious for the last four days." I pause and take another sip of the oh-so-delightful coffee.

"Last night, at 11:38pm a boggle and two Menacing Hobs broke into the Janet Annenberg Hooker Hall of Geology, Gems, and Minerals within the Smithsonian National Museum of Natural History – they killed two guards, critically injured a third, and made off with a necklace valued at over eleven million pounds; erm, roughly thirteen million dollars. Which, while ridiculously luxe to most, is far less than the Hooker Emeralds, Whitney Flame Topaz or Hope Diamond are worth – even on the black market – all of which are housed in the same display."

"I see how this would be distressing," Nomer, cagey, sips at her coffee and holds my gaze level with hers. Blessed Cybele, those silver eyes are daunting when they focus on you like that.

"While a Fae crime, here or up in DC is no nevermind to this court," I stress her role to show my hand and the gravity. "The incidents seem to be connected with one another and, in-turn, connected with Carterburg's history." I feel Tam tense beside me as I continue, "Aside from the Lares' stolen papers and injury, the only damage at the scene was to one of the paintings in the Records Hall; a portrait of Lord and Lady Stuart – specifically, great claw marks tore through the canvas at Lucy Stuart's neck."

I can't help but notice Nomer and Phuc both flinch at the woman's name.

"What was stolen from the Smithsonian?" Phuc's dark brow is raised in what almost looks like trepidatious concern. His voice is nowhere near its usual melodious timbre.

"The London-Stuart Egg: a gorgeous white-gold necklace of intricately-cut small diamonds and white sapphires laced around a large, oval-cut diamond."

I can't be sure, Tam has a better view from where he's sitting between us – I'll have to ask him later – but I think that Phuc just clutched at Nomer's hand as I described the gem.

"The necklace – which, incidentally, is the selfsame one whose image was slashed in the attack – was donated by Lady Stuart in 1928, bequeathed to the Smithsonian in her last months. Her last public outing was its debut and for months afterwards rumors flew about Washington that the gem was 'Faerie Curst' as often as it was said to be 'Faerie Blest'. From what HRH Mabh and Taliesin have said," *which is not all of what needs-be, not by a long shot, if I know them. And I do.* "The gem was not gifted to Lucy at the end of her service to the crown, neither of Them knowing its true provenance. I suspect, and you can call it feline intuition, that wherever this diamond came from, it wasn't an African or Indian diamond mine."

I set my lamentably empty cup back down and smile broadly while I pour more. Watching them both as I do, I get ready to play my card. If this burgeoning friendship and camaraderie between the Selighe Court and the Court of Blood and Glitter is to make any headway, I have to be as forthright as possible.

"I had hoped that you might know more, Phuc."

Forthright, but not naïve.

"Tomorrow, Tam and I are off to DC to view the tapes and interview the surviving guards. But, beforehand, I wanted to know all that I could; the scant reports gleaned from Carterburg's finest and the Hollow Hill's library left me in the same spot I started in. I figured that if anyone in-town would know more – and be up front about it – it would be you, Phuc. You've been here since the beginning; since the first faeries and Fae started streaming across the veils. As Tam already had plans to be here tonight, I thought 'Why not try?' … and so, here we are."

Tam smiles encouragingly, giving a thumbs up beneath his saucer.

I know they mean to be subtle, years of friendship distill their silent communication, but I'd have to be in another room to miss it – Phuc's glances and Nomer's grimaces – as they seem to weigh just how to answer; Cybele, I pray that their better natures win out.

"You were correct in your guess," Phuc finally responds, holding his eyes on Nomer. "I can guess its origin; at least, its origin on this side of the veils."

It's a gem of Faerie? I mean, that would explain a lot, but … Metrokoites.

"But, first, let me tell you of its broader history – its context," he paused and took a deep breath; like the ones you do before a dive into dark and frigid waters.

"As you've probably guessed, the initial reaction of mortalkind in Carterburg to the Fae influx was … less than pleasant. What I'm – what we're," he looked again to Nomer, "about to tell you is a history painful and seldom spoken of; but it is true all the more for it."

The Puca's golden eyes squeeze shut in anguish and I almost regret having to ask.

4

"After faeries were visibly seen stepping through the veils into the mortal world of 1871, during a city-wide celebration at Ferry Farm no less, a mad commotion and confusion reigned in Carterburg for weeks on end. Two Hobs and a dryad died – while a dozen other Fae were injured – at the hands of the panicked mob," Phuc intoned.

"Finally, a Town Council was called almost a month into our being here. Worries and voices were heard and addressed on both sides of the matter and – after a rather ugly affair pretending itself a debate – finally, a 'solution' was put forth by one of the city's leading families. Laucks Island: the many-acred tongue of rock and forest on the Stefford side of the river, it lies just past the Falmouth bridge."

In all the years I've lived and worked within elfshot of it, I don't think I've ever visited the place; I know of Scotts Island, it's the small spit of brush and rock that allows the Chatham bridge to safely span Hedgeman's river, but Laucks?

"It wasn't an unappealing place for there were young trees and thick grass, vines and a thin grove of apple trees; the Hedgeman's water flowed about it beautifully in thick eddies and whorls – back then it was more field and farm than shadowy woods and bracken. At its head was a many-roomed stone-and brick manse. When we voiced our concerns, wanting the freedom the expanse of Midgard had promised, we were firmly met with mortal opposition; it was 'for our own safety', 'Who knows how others will react to you' they said … and for the next two years most of the faerie brethren were sequestered there."

Seldom in the annals of man or Faerie has this ever been done with genuine concern for others.

"While a few chose to try and live freely in wood and river," he continued. "More still were 'civilized' and wanted for hearth and home; they who remembered days of mortal/Fae households in concert and hoped a repeat."

Beside me, Tam has leaned forward, a rapt and almost heartsore look playing on his face as he reaches out to gently hold Phuc's hand. The gesture, well-meant and heartfelt, pauses the Puca and an amber warmth dances at the rim of his golden eyes.

"Few of us had come with much, if any, of money or valuables and enough mortals knew better than to trust to Faerie Gold freely given. Instead of living homeless in the streets, subject to the unkind and sometimes violent whims of passersby, we were 'offered to earn our way' with payable work on the island so that, when the time came, we could live as 'productive members of society'. It was no less than indentured servitude; brute labor – farming, working the vines and mill on the island, or tending the small manse at its head for next-to-nothing pay. With their little war over, *someone* had to do it; in the confusion of faeries' reality, the city was slow to recognize our rights and *they* took advantage of that."

"Fuck iad," Tam's eyes are glowing, an electric blue fizzle while the distinct odor of ozone seeps about. "What right do they have?"

"None, but they gave themselves the right, the permission, and – in the end – the absolution for what happened," Nomer spoke up for the first time. A thin haze of silvery energy dances along her long nails as she absently taps the teak chest on her desk.

I knew those first years were rough – faerie and mortal coexistence has been a long, occasionally ugly, road over the millennia; the main reason Mabh created Faerie and pulled us apart from humanity – but, Hecate, I hadn't realized it had been this bad.

Nowhere was this written in official Court records, nor have I heard any speak of it before; it's almost unreal to think of it happening, but I can see no lies in Phuc's face or his voice. The pain, the grief, the memory of it is real and undeniable.

"I'm so sorry – I know that seems inadequate, but-"

"It's in the past," Phuc waves me off, his smile thin but warm, as he continues.

"It wasn't until the first hundred or so had been gathered – mostly Hobs, but a few of us 'greater' Fae – that we found our strength again and remembered who we were: mortalkind's neighbors, not their slaves."

I can see the resolute pain in Phuc's eyes; hear it in his voice as he strains.

"I'd be lying if I said I regretted the bloodshed, Circe, but it was necessary; I do not regret it although I sorrow for it. Look in their history books," his words are clipped, almost sharp. "You will find no mention of any of it; not of their deeds nor ours – a silence fraught with remorse and denial. But, in the twilight gloam of a summer's even, the manse – its master and his cruel wife – and its vines burned while we looked on. No songs, no cheers – no pity for the dead, but no celebration of it, either. Even today, you will not find a gravemarker for either of them and mortal scholars do wonder at what happened in those early years, but find no answers."

Pausing to sip at his tea, I can almost taste the weariness in Phuc as he tells us this story – this history; his history.

"Herkyna and I, with a few others, established new ground rules with the city over the next few months and our envoy – the inestimable Mme Greenteeth herself – returned with the beginnings of Royal contact and forgiveness for our return to mortal lands, exiled from Her presence in name, but not spirit."

This much I remember; it was a long discussion in the Queene's Privy Council – heated and emotional – on *how* and *what* to do about 'The Carterburg situation' finally ending with the tentative role of it as neutral ground.

"What was the family's name," Tam's quiet question fills the room.

"Stuart."

It feels like the oxygen has left the space and stars dance behind my eyes.

"The fuck?!" Tam succinctly, if not crassly, sums it up.

"Brendan Stuart, and his wife Cathryn – forgotten by history, but not by those who were there, silent as we are – were swiftly explained to the Fae as 'underhanded' and 'scoundrels' who'd done these wicked deeds unapproved and unknown. Even the Governor stepped all over himself to rewrite the situation, claiming that Stuart had lied to the city as smoothly as he'd lied to the Fae."

"But, but why the silence – why haven't we heard any of this before now," Tam asks – concern and anguish plainly on his face and in his voice.

"The closest I've likened it," Phuc turns to him, "is to when a wounded animal, afraid of the trap that caught its leg, warily still hunts the brush for food for it needs to live."

Tam's skeptical eye matches my own opinion.

"We came through the veils to escape –the rules of Faerie Monarchy, personal, professional, or any one of a thousand reasons, but, each of us came to escape *something* in Faerie and that >need< for freedom of Faerie overrode our fears of what we found here. Plus, despite the escape, far too few survivors of Laucks Island and the Stuarts thereon lived past 1890. Oh, some were trundled off to private residences like the Stuarts' manse in White Oak, but, a noticeable number died of 'mysterious yet explainable' circumstances in the intervening years. A scarce handful of us still live, fewer still call Carterburg home. Silence and private grudges seemed the best course; silence and hopeful forgetfulness."

Behind her desk, Nomer's sharply beautiful face is a mask of unreadable mystery as these unspoken tragedies are laid bare; although, behind her, flickers of violet and onyx Glamour dance erratically – mesmerizingly – and I start when Phuc resumes his narration.

"Lucy Stuart, one of the last surviving children of the immediate Stuart family, entered a proposed seven-year service tithe to the Queene in the summer of 1881, seven years almost to the day after the death of her brother on Laucks Island," *after protracted and exhausting negotiations with the Queene,* I silently add, remembering the boldness of the family's requests.

"In 1888, more than a year shy of the end of her contract, she was returned – with money and renewed land – by the Queene of Faerie, where she took up caring for her ailing grandmother for the next few years."

This part of the story has always niggled at me; worrying at my whiskers like a gnat. Mabh has never given me more than veiled comments and hidden, layered nuances – despite my role as Her investigator and our kinship.

It's always left me curious; doubly moreso after investigating the death of Lucy's great granddaughter on the Faerie-gift property. Mabh would change the subject, if not avoid it outright, when any question of *that* possible connection would pop up.

Whatever could Lucy have done in service to the Queene to warrant such?

"In the years she served Mabh," Nomer's icy tone nearly matches the frigid silver of her eyes. "Her family, 'impoverished' – in their estimation, but still rather well-off by any other's standards – extorted the Fae who sought a hearth in their tenements. When Lucy returned, although favorable to Fae, she did little to change it until her parents' death in 1894 when, with her husband, she firmly took the family and company's reigns. While she may have been better than them," Nomer's words slice the air, "she was the aberration in that family, not the norm; she, too, made choices forgivable and unforgiveable."

"Yes. Although they presented a kindly face, welcoming Fae – or at least our money – and asked few questions, the Stuarts were … oh," Phuc scrunched his brow. "What is it they call them on telly?"

"Slum lords?" Tam adds, his face stony.

"Yes, that's it," he turns back to me, his mahogany cheeks drawn in the intensity of his mood.

"The upkeep on most of their properties was beyond lax; the indoor plumbing only existed in the warehouses-cum-brownstones of the upper stretch. Sadly, theirs weren't the worst of the offerings in those days; although, they were already calling the stretch where we gathered the Fae District."

"It was positively Medieval in comparison to the rest of town," Nomer's jaw, tight, matches her tone. "At least, until the elder Stuarts died; things really began to change when Mabh and the Selighe Court finally had our backs," catching my eye, she softens somewhat. "No offense, Enchantress."

"None taken – Tam and I were two of the too-few voices imploring Her Majesty to do as much sooner; that it happened is good, but, I'm sorry it took so long."

Nodding, and catching sight of the flickering Glamours behind her, Nomer finally seems to still and breathe more easily.

"We give you the breadth of this background, unspoken but to a few – and remembered by even fewer; we trust you to use your discretion with it."

"S'cat's honor," I hold up my hand and nod my head towards the pair as Tam does the same.

"We tell you all of this because it has to do with your question," Phuc continued, standing and coming to lean against the great desk with Nomer behind him and to his right.

"You see, I remember the stone – its like is not common regardless of the age of man; a great oval-cut diamond the size of a quail's egg, clear as a summer's day and thrice as bright. It arrived with an emigrating Fae after Mabh had begun talks with Carterburg, he brought it with him from the Northern reaches of Faerie; it was one of several treasures he'd wisely carried across the veils. He used it to secure lodging in one of the Stuarts' brownstones, on the hill-end I believe. Like with so many of their other dealings with Fae – outside of the Royal Court, that is," he adds, his voice wry and weary. "They did their best to wring what they could and deliver as little as possible: in the end, they gave him a fraction of its worth although it still set him up with basics for the entirety of his stay."

I nod, as I pull up the file on the gem from my tablet.

"A few years later, in 1891, at the behest of her parents the renowned jewel smith, Robhwyn London, re-set it with the lacework of metal and stones," I add, cementing the connection.

"As the first and only Lady Stuart, yes. Embellishing it to pretend – to add such airs – they had the right of it, calling themselves Gentry of Faerie," Phuc's tone is fairly acidic at this.

"It was all pretense; the Queene never actually granted the title, nor – as I recall – did Lucy ever wish Her to," Tam adds, surely remembering Lucy's timid nature.

"True, that stemmed from her parents – but, she didn't stop them."

Also true. Lucy was a meek sort, kindly and well-meaning, but would defer to whichever authority was nearest – be it royalty or familial. Knowing something of her family's behavior now, this doesn't surprise me.

From behind, Nomer leans forward and gently wraps her long fingers around Phuc's wrist, silently calming him; strengthening him. Turning his horned brow, I try not to eavesdrop as he silently mouths his thanks.

I smile encouragement at Nomer as she supports him.

In our repeated dealings over the last decades, I don't think I've ever seen his mood so frayed; his emotions so raw.

Sometimes I forget that he isn't merely a handsome Puca who spends his time DJing or telling stories, he's nearly as mythic as I am and a Fae of both profound passions and deep strengths; strengths that nurse old wounds and keep them close. I wonder, and I worry, about what all he endured – what happened to him and those other Fae – in those two years? Part of me wants to ask, the curiosity tingling through to my fingertips; were I in my accustomed form, my tail would be lashing. Instead, I focus on the whole of it, instead of the details, and reach for the tray on the desk.

"This lines up," I dangle a fourth biscuit between my fingers as I try to steer the enlightening, if not potentially contentious, conversation back. "The Lares woke up earlier today; he's banged up – crack on the head, hairline fracture, internal bleeding, and a severe concussion – so, even with wyrmroot, blüdmoss, and round-the-clock ministrations from Klepios, he won't be leaving hospital for at least another week."

And, after my short visit, Taliesin and I made sure that he is to have no visitors and an around-the-clock guard of Royal Korvu at his door. Armed and uninterested in quibbles.

"Although a bit addled and rather terrified, he was able to give a clear testimony of the night; he was researching the Stuart family for [**REDACTED**] –*dammit, I hate it when She does that* – having found an error in accounts when the shadows came alive. His description of the boggle and Menacing Hobs matches what the initial report from the Smithsonian gave us: of a woman, scantily but elegantly clad, with a skull head and long black hair. They scared the shite out of him, causing him to slip – while he was unconscious, they must have stolen the papers where he found these story irregularities, beat the living tar out of him, and then slashed the painting before disappearing."

"My guess, Circe, is that he stumbled onto a piece of what we just told you."

"I wouldn't be surprised, Phuc. My only hope is that, finding these malefactors, we also find those papers and his reports – tying everything up into a nice little bundle."

"When was the last time that happened?"

I don't even dignify Tam's question with anything other than a raised brow and quiet raspberry.

"Were they freelance or Unselighe?" Nomer's eyes pin me.

"Unselighe, from his description of her scent."

All three give me quizzical looks and I'm about to answer when a firm rapping at the door pulls us all from the conversation. I'm sure we look like a pack of meerkats, eyes wide and staring as the wards glitter away, when The Lady Ophelia – a glittering beard and body-suit of tattoos set against a gorgeous couture take on a ringmaster's get-up – steps through the door.

"'Scuse me, Blo – oh, hey everyone – but, Orielle snagged me as I was heading to the stage: the hen party is making a scene and she thought it best that either you 'handle it or we let loose some drunk Corbies on their dumb asses' – her words, not mine. Personally, I'd say let them, but … " the elegant gold-and-crimson queen shrugs her indifference towards the rowdy group's comfort.

It's obvious how she stands on their impropriety and I can't say I honestly blame her; I know how obnoxious they can get.

"If you'll excuse me, Circe, boys, I won't be but a moment."

The usual cool tone is there, but, beneath the Glamour and finery you can almost see the stressed and worry-sore young man as his gaze lingers on Phuc.

"Nomer – Blodeuwedd – please," standing, I set my cup (empty again *sigh*) on the side table and incline my head. "Please; we've already taken up enough of your evening. That you and Phuc have been this helpful is …" I have trouble rounding the words, my hands fumbling in midair. "It's more than I could have hoped."

A smile tugs through the make-up and brightens the Glamour about Nomer as she inclines her own bewigged height. Phuc, too, weakly smiles and nods at me as he joins her.

"It is our pleasure," she lays her porcelain hand on Phuc's shoulder as Tam and I precede them towards the door. "Don't be a stranger, Enchantress – you either, Little Boy Blue."

As we follow Ophelia into the bright-lit hall, Tam chuckling at the nicknames, I turn backwards to thank them again and stop myself short.

Through the shadowy Glamours dancing about the door, I glimpse the pair standing stock still in the middle of the room. Thankfully, although not in cat shape, I am able to silently back away before either notice.

Phuc, leaning against her, is quietly sobbing.

5

Official Court Investigator Case File (Supplemental) -

February 4th

Tam is late.

I'd say that I'm surprised, but, I'd be more surprised if he weren't.

In all fairness, it was a late night for him – for us both.

After we went our separate ways, him to another date with Simon (out until at least three) and my happy ass back to the Hollow Hill, I stayed up late trying to piece together any records from those first years over belated sushi and white wine. Be it City official documentation, op-eds or articles in the Carterburg Post, or even confidential Court files nothing panned out.

It's like a gap in time.

Oh, there were articles and notes – mundane little things of absolute inconsequence (new beau monde fashions and the like); but nothing in *anything* I could get my paws on did so much as hint about the larger goings-on. One article in the Post mentioned the astonishing appearance of the Faery Folk at a celebration for George Washington, but, between that one in 1871 and the 1874 articles concerning the talk of the new Fae District … absolutely nothing of note.

I may have knocked the wine glass off of the table – backhanding it – in a fit of feline picque before sauntering off for a long soak in a hot bath.

END FILE

....

"Well, well, well – look who decided to join me at the ripe hour of," I mime looking at the nonexistent watch on my wrist, "almost eleven-thirty in the morning."

"Hey, sorry – but, a work of art like my famous spit curl takes time."

"Famous? More like infamous, Tam," I flick my fingertips through the looser strands near his temple.

"Plus, I snagged *Hearthstone* coffee on my way up," he hands me a travel cup of steaming, delight. "Forgive me?"

They do a lovely Darjeeling/espresso mix whose musky spiciness is so strong it practically curls my fur ... and I love it.

"... for now," I smile between sips.

I may have a coffee problem.

Appearing between the airs beside me, Tamlinn managed to arrive only twenty seven minutes late; his hair, in his defense, looks great and the coffee more than makes up for it. The dark waves and curl are nearly black against his creamy skin and bright blue eyes; he's dressed in form-fitting jeans and a pewter-blue t-shirt and opened button-up beneath a stormy pea coat. Of the two of us, he looks closer to the detective.

Since I was told to "play nice, wear a human face – we don't need a great, bluddy cat waltzing through the museum giving mortal folk heart attacks" (Taliesin's words, not mine), and I can't splay my fang or claw, I settle for a more intimidating look than my general gingery-champagne aesthetic.

Instead of the summery glow of golden cheek and honeyed hair, I sport sharper angles and darker tones; purposefully evoking the more aggressive and villainous artistic interpretations of me.

Corvine-black waves and curls are pulled back into a ponytail while a few wisps and frizzy ringlets escape the coif, framing my face and softening my Doric nose and proud, Cretan chin; that those curls end in glittering ginger brightness is my business. Golden, feathery horns twine and curl backwards, star-bright against the black of my hair and shimmering into the thickest part of the ponytail. My Helios-kissed tan and olive features are drawn in, my smile less full; and my eyes are the green of a sickly moon whose glow is reflected from the depths of the Adriatic.

I opted for pragmatic over fashion when I paired dark jeans and a turtleneck (pine green and made from Auroch yarn) with a scarf of eldritch greens and iridescent beads. My sensible riding boots and a thick coat of summer's twilight (and warm Glamour-treated wool, natch) hopefully tie it all together.

The coat isn't wholly decorative as, despite my general Fae-resistance to the cold, I'm no fan of the wet chill that rests here in the tidal basin. Turning away from the lamppost and thin trees, here at the edge of the National Mall, I take another sip of the coffee and tug my collar higher against the damnably damp and constantly-biting wintry wind of a Washington DC morning.

"Shall we?"

"I thought you'd never ask, 'Little Boy Blue,'" I smile, teasingly.

"Hey, I've been called worse, Enchantress."

"Same," I slowly steer us between milling mortals taking snapshots of, and selfies in front of, the tall, imposing buildings that surround us; barely missing a bicyclist who, head down, bore little to no concern for the pedestrians in his way.

"How was the rest of your night; you had another date with Simon didn't you?"

The light blush dancing along Tam's tapered ears confirms it moments before his words, "Yeah – another night of dancing, making out, and eating ridiculous amounts of food before saying our goodnights in the wee hours."

I (barely) refrain from giggling at the tone of his voice. "I'm glad; this is the longest I've known you to date anyone in – what, centuries?"

"He's the first guy since Trev that I've even thought that there could be *more* with, y'know?"

I nod as we maneuver through more sight-seers.

"I'll admit, the age thing isn't >*as*< weird to me as it was a few months ago – honestly, at our ages there will always be some form of significant gap. I mean, it's still weird, but seeing you two together, you bring out the best in each other; he gets this sober and eerily older-than-he-looks energy behind his eyes when you're together and ..." I stop to sip the coffee and order my words.

"I can't remember seeing you being as relaxed as when you're together and you're not looking. Does that make sense?"

I hope that, despite the caffeine-induced word vomit I'm coming across as supportive, not judgmental. "It's like you drop the carefree role of Courtier and the stoic aloofness of Elf Knight behind you and you're just Tam. Not Tamlinn or Tam of the Blue and Queene's Blade; just Tam the friend and boyfriend."

"I swear to Cybele, 'Cee you're too sweet for words," he pauses to kiss my forehead. "Don't worry; your reputation is safe with me." The conspiratorial glint to word and glance is pure rake.

A stiff breeze ruffles scarf and branch while we slowly pass wintry bare cherry trees.

Taking the moment, my voice sotto and my curiosity sopra, "You've never answered me, though; did you ever figure out that odd otherness about Simon?"

"Ahhh, there's the other shoe dropping – and the detective I call my best friend," his voice is jovial, nonetheless I can't help wondering if I should have waited … but, there's no taking it back now. "No, I've never answered you about it, and yes; I did figure it out. At least, I think I did."

My confusion has to be written across my arched brow.

"When he was a kid, Simon had an accident – fell out of a tree, it was a nasty business – and lost a lot of blood; there's a nasty scar along the bottom of his chin down his throat almost to his Adams apple. Apparently, he has an odd blood type and the first donor match was a faerie; which 1) implies that he potentially has Fae ancestry and 2) explains the fey-esque otherness. A transfusion wouldn't necessarily produce that lingering effect that he has, but it might enhance recessive … *traits*."

It might, but damn; that's still a rather convenient, albeit plausible, explanation. Changing tacks, and dropping the topic (for now), I steer us back towards the original conversation and the vast building ahead.

"I'll confess; I am genuinely intrigued by Nomer; both as the young man beneath the make-up, conflictingly kind and bitter, and as the enigmatic midnight queen who suddenly holds a sanctioned throne of Faerie."

"Speaking of new changes," Tam tucks his arm about me as another bicyclist barrels down the rime-touched path; his tone conversational, but back to business.

"We've investigated Blodeuwedd, Miss Nomer, in proximal association with, what, a dozen cases and incidents over the last thirty years? True, most of them had more to do with The Phosphorescent's antics in and around *The Crossroads* itself more than with him; but, it's legit wild how things have turned around so swiftly."

He's right; despite, or perhaps due to our longevity, Fae are slow to change (if we ever do), and the seeming change of heart with Miss Nomer – with *Blodeuwedd* – has left us both on uncertain footing. Obviously, from what they told us last night, there's more to Blodeuwedd's past here in Carterburg than meets the eye. I'd have to be a newborn kitten to miss the raw pain when Nomer spoke of the Stuarts and their treatment of Fae; while Phuc's anguish was on display, they both did a conspicuous misdirect on Blodeuwedd's.

There's definitely more yet that they didn't tell us.

The fact that I've found myself growing fond of our burgeoning friendship these last two months – Blodeuwedd's pervasive curiosity and adoration for bitter, bitter black coffee rival my own – complicates things all the more.

Truth is, it wasn't until last year, when he helped us at Ravensclere, that even the >hints< of something other than a venal, uninterested drag queen lay beneath the make-up.

And now?

In the short span of a year and change he's shown more – he sent me word, anonymously of course, on how and where to find The Phosphorescent (allowing us to effectively remove them from the board as a conclusive threat to Fae and mortal safety); he directly intervened in the Androphagoi incident, and has done his best at providing a truly safe haven for all outsiders within his walls.

Yes, many of these moves had less-than altruistic motives – I'd be a fool to assume he didn't have a beef with Corbyn, and Nomer told me herself that she loathed Lugh and Nemedh for what they did at Ravensclere – but, their good shouldn't be excised by that.

And when he, when *she*, and Phuc took their stand with Huginn and Muninn that night, drastically shifting the pieces across the board?

Well, the picture became a bit clearer.

Blodeuwedd, beneath the paint and Glamours, doesn't just dislike the generality and formal rigidity of Faerie Courts and their rules; he loathes the Unselighe Court and its royalty with a bone-breaking will.

Which, much as with that first cup of coffee, it's as good a place to start as any. Even if I can't wholly believe the incomplete pictures she paints, I can trust that hate.

But, the meat and gristle of it?

I >want< to believe Blodeuwedd.

"Can you believe those shitheads," Tam jerks his thumb back at the receding bicyclists, a third now careening down the Mall towards his friends and a small family left shaken in his wake, as I realize I hadn't answered him; lost in the labyrinths of my own thoughts.

"It isn't easy, Tam, but, I think – so far – Blodeuwedd and Nomios have been on the up-and-up with us."

"We-ell, at least up-and-to-the-side with us; intrigue and plotting seem second nature to Nomer. But, I think you're right – they may be holding back things, but, I don't think they're lying to us." Nodding as we step across the trickling traffic in front of the museum, Tam finishes. "Something tells me, I don't think they will – not about anything that impacts us or innocents – either."

"Agreed," I smile and take another long sip of the coffee as we make our way up the wide, limestone steps towards the museum's formal entrance.

I've always enjoyed the Roman-esque theatre that the Smithsonian's Natural History building embodies; the crisscross grating within the glass – both in door and in window, the beautiful marble and limestone arches and lintels reaching skywards, the columns parading down either side in marshal fortitude, and, of course, that incredible dome who whispers secrets to the earth and sky.

If I half-close my eyes and look upwards at the Pantheon-esque façade, I can almost pretend I'm somewhere – somewhen – else.

"Ma'am?"

A thick-set and balding father, his wife and children in-tow – the family who'd narrowly avoided collision with that last bicyclist, stand almost on my coattails; they're either about to bum rush or plow me down in their haste to get in.

Stepping to the side, my coffee almost spilling in my eagerness to avoid their stampede, Tam and I wait and slip in through the revolving door; letting the tourist-y brood pass ahead of us.

"Good morning, madam – sir," a young Black man, his uniform crisp and his smile genuine, greets us as we stop just past the screenings, the vast coffered rotunda filled-to-teeming with mortals and its taxidermy'd elephant – 'Jumbo' if my memory serves – ahead of us. "How can we help you?"

"I'm Detective Kay Invidiosa, and this is my associate Tam Linn; we're here to meet with your commander regarding," I lower my voice, "the theft of the London-Stuart Egg."

Tam rolls his eyes beside me at my choice of a nom de l'enquêteur.

For some reason, mortals don't react well to singular names – outside of Madonna, Cher, and Björk that is – so, I tend to use whatever name springs to mind. And, as that viciously-accurate Waterhouse painting was the inspiration for today's look … here we are.

"Certainly, miss – if you'll be so kind as to wait," he gestures towards the grand desk ahead of us, where tourists and sightseers mill about with pamphlets. "Captain Wolsh will be with you in a few."

"You Glamoured our coffee to be invisible, didn't you?" I whisper, as we walk over. "He didn't say word-one about it."

"Why get hot coffee if we have to chug it or ditch it immediately?"

Fair point.

Pulling up the tablet from my Hermes pocket, I surreptitiously take a long swig behind it and lean against a bare corner free of flyers, visitors, docents, and touch screen consoles. While it's not quite that beautiful blend that *The Crossroads* crew brew, it's some damn fine java.

"Good morning, Enchantress – Little Boy Blue."

I practically choke on the coffee, snorting and laughing around it in a most unladylike way and, beside me, Tam is practically laughing himself into an asthma attack.

"What the … ?"

Standing before us – garbed in a smartly-tailored and low-cut suit of black (its fabric gleaming deep purple and indigo where the light hits it), crisp arched heels, sunglasses (despite the fact that we're indoors) over over-the-top smoky eyes, and a charcoal coat of (hopefully faux) fox fur draping off his slim shoulders – and practically laughing at the spectacle, is Blodeuwedd.

Until now, I don't think I've ever actually seen him truly out of drag – let alone out in 'the real world' away from magic, monsters, and faerie bars.

"What in Hecate's third butt cheek are you doing here?"

Raising his brow, and lowering the shades to reveal his hoary eyes surrounded by artfully applied shadows, he taps the large, bronze plaque beside my elbow with a black-painted nail, and smiles.

"These updates to our visitor services were made possible by the generosity of," I read, stopping at the third name down, "Blodeuwedd."

"Somehow I never thought you concerned yourself with mortal affairs inside Carterburg, let alone outside."

"A few years ago," the pale Faerie smiles at Tam and points to the closed off wing to our right, "the museum approached Nomios about possibly working together on an installation regarding the early history of Man and Faerie – the sort of stuff your handsome friend Toby writes about. Perhaps he's mentioned it?"

I almost laugh as Tam sputters in surprise; it's true, he's been one of Professor Tobias "Toby" O'Connor's main sources on middle Faerie history during the Medieval and post-Roman eras (inside Faerie as well as on earth); over the last two years he's done a dozen interviews and helped him pool conflicting histories by combing The Hollow Hill's expansive library. I guess, despite the semi-constant contact, Prof O'Connor managed to avoid mentioning his involvement here; I know this is certainly the first I've heard of it.

"While it's only now just begun actual installation, I thought it prudent to financially ensure *that* it happened. As Carterburg's premiere Fae-ce," he pauses on the pun just long enough for Tam to groan and laugh, recovering from the jibe. "Nomios and I thought it in our best interest to remain involved before, during, and after. Which is why, for the last few years, I – well, *The Crossroads* itself – have been a decent donor and 'friend' to the museum."

Add one more puzzling side to the queen – philanthropist.

"When you mentioned the theft last night, I'll confess my curiosity was piqued, and when you said you were coming today, well …" he gestures elegantly, his coat swinging wide and theatrically, taking the whole of the scene in with his long, tapered fingers. "Here we are."

Here we are indeed.

"Sirs, ma'am," the young guard has returned. "It seems that Captain Wolsh is indisposed at the moment – he's still across the block with the FBI answering some basics about the theft; I'm so sorry. He shouldn't be more than another half-an-hour or so if you don't mind waiting."

"We do," Blodeuwedd smiles, handsome and flirtatious with a silvery wink, "but that won't stop us." He air kisses the space beside the young man's cheek causing him to immediately flush; seeing Blodeuwedd like this is both enlightening and confusing (an effect I doubt he's unaware of). "If the good captain gets here before we return, we'll be wandering in Western Civilization – I'm sure your little cameras will be able to find us."

Linking his long arms between us, he begins to steer us away from the desk; glamorous, and Glamoured coffee besides, to get immediately lost amongst the throngs of sightseers.

"He was cute – well-meaning and earnest; three qualities I admire but hold in little regard outside of a pet."

"I was wondering – you did seem to be laying it on a bit thickly back there," I half-whisper as we thread our way towards the grand staircase off to the back-and-right of us.

"Yes. Yes I was."

Ahhh. Enigmatic – that's the Blodeuwedd I'm far more used to.

"In the art of misdirection, Enchantress, giving them exactly what they hope to see – a flamboyant, over-the-top, ebullient, and heavily flirtatious gay man – allows me to do whatever the Hels I wish beneath their gaze. If I'd wanted to, I could have, say," he produces an electronic card in-between his fingers, "made a Glamoured copy of the guard's pass-key as a just-in-case."

The card vanishes in rainbow sparks – whether into his breast pocket or the aether, I'm not quite sure.

"In this case, though – what it allowed me to do was steal you both away and get a private word in."

No longer arm in arm, we casually take the stairs as Blodeuwedd continues. "Whether he's aware of it or not (and, judging from his open face and manner, he's not), his boss – a bruiser and 'retired' District Detective – is at the FBI building

searching for a way to avoid working with you, not answering any routine questions about the theft."

I wish this surprised me.

All-too frequently I've noticed a distinct lack of willingness by law enforcement to work with, what many sheriffs and police perceive as a threat by way of, 'private law' folk. I hate to rain on their parade, but, Tam and I are every bit the officers of the law as they; it's simply that we serve a different court of law, a separate government.

Sadly, more often than not, we're met with scowls and bruised egos instead of smiles and open dialogues. I was really hoping that this time would be different.

6

"Seriously, were Ancient Greeks really that short?"

Turning, I see the hand painted figures of a man and woman against the wall, with placards noting their average heights as 5'7" and 5'3" respectively.

"I mean, that's accurate; although, it's not >that< short."

"Enchantress, I mean," Blodeuwedd chuckled and went to stand next to them, his raised brow almost lost to his dark hair: Even in the flat dress shoes he's wearing, he stands nearly a foot above their heads.

"Okay, you have a point. Although, if you want to talk shorter, the Minoans in our heyday; even the men were slim and lithe in shape, but they topped out at about here," I gesture to the spot near my lower earlobe, about 5'6". "While they were by and large more hospitable and friendly, as compared to the Doric and Achaean men, I tended to go for the tall, dark and handsome sort of mortals – Faerie blest regardless, so my opinions maa-aay be a tad biased there."

"I, too, prefer a gentleman to be of an imposing … height," said with a wink, Blodeuwedd manages to make that sound positively indecent.

We killed the first half-an-hour meandering about the second floor with no clear path or goal. Along the way, we skirted past the closed portion of the gem hall where the theft occurred – of course, I let a small spying cantrip slip past the walled barricade. It showed us what remained of the crime scene – they've yet to remove the tape outline of one guard or suitably clean up the blood splatters – and proved that they were treating it as if just another mortal crime.

More's the pity.

As we leaned against the balcony's railing, people watching, examining the cantrip's footage on my tablet and waiting for the crowd to thin about the Western Civilization entrance, a young woman seemed to hover in the periphery. Perky, pale, and brunette, she was doing everything she could not to attract our attention as she waited to … attract our attention.

"Methinks you have an admirer, your majesty," Tam tapped Blodeuwedd on the furred collar, subtly pointing to the young woman.

With a well-contained (from the girl's vantage, anyways) sigh, Blodeuwedd dropped the sunglasses and waved the young woman over.

"Homigoddt, I fucking love you. My friends and I have been to your shows like, a thousand times."

Somehow, I doubt that number quite matches up, but, she's Blodeuwedd's fan, his problem. Not my circus, not my hyperventilating white girl.

"How very kind of you – I hope you've tipped the girls well and patted a fair few spandexed bums when they cross your path."

The blush that spread across her cheeks says she may have.

"Would it be okay – I mean, I know you're not in geish or anything, but, would you? Could I?"

"Take a photo?" Surprised by his question, the young woman almost nonstop babbled trying to get the phone out of her purse.

The longer I'm around the queen, I'm learning to differentiate the levels of nuance in Blodeuwedd's nearly monotone delivery; for example, right now from his question (and brow), he's somewhere between *mildly amused* and *'hurry up and finish, I have things to do' irritated*.

"Here, allow me," Tam deftly swooped in to snag the phone and take the picture of the elphin girl and the monolithic not-in-drag drag queen.

"Flash on, please – auto is not on; auto is a Nifl-damned lie."

After two (successful?) photos, Tam handed the phone back as she giggled and smiled.

"Thank you, I mean – so seriously, thank you. I love you. It's because of you that I'm so into Voguing right now," she word-vomited as she backed away, getting lost in the crowd.

After that, we all-but ran – silently laughing – into the Western Civilization wing. We've wandered around its entirety over the last (*additional*) half-an-hour (*yes, I'm counting*); beginning in Paleolithic times before eventually making our way to the Greek and Roman area. There is something awfully disquieting about seeing your history naked and splayed for the consumption of an audience.

The krater and kálux on display to my right feature classic white and black slip imagery of 'The cunning goddess and sorceress Circe, bewitching Odysseus' men' and 'Odysseus blinding the Cyclops' [they never did get my nose right]; while the large granite Sphynx and Caryatid pieces a few feet away were from a temple in Boeotia I remember being constructed (the sculptor's men were kind and left tithes and offerings to the Fae). The broken gorgoneion above me is from a small village on the Black Sea near fallen Colchis; and the bronze and chalcedony jewelry in the case I'm leaning over?

Were carved as talisman of the Fae – you can just make out the elongated ears beneath the time-worn gloss of the stone. On its obverse, and shown as a photo, is "an obscure prayer to what researchers assume are the Eumenides", end quote. The entreaty, "Watch over and do not look too closely" is a reference to the 'Kindly Ones', one of the many names ancient mortals would call us; both naming us in their power and hoping to deflect our attention. It was a common enough prayer asking for our favor – generally the Androdoroi and almost never the Androphagoi, but fell out of use by the 9th century BCE in the aftermath of our mass exodus to Faerie.

"If the habits of mortals in the Ancient World are that intriguing to you," I turn back to Blodeuwedd. "Why don't you ask Phuc about them? From what I know of his own, storied history, *the* Nomios Phuc could tell many a tale of forgotten lore."

And he could.

Last night, after my petulant fit and bath – curled up in frustration, I went back through my oldest diaries searching through millennia old notes and memories in the hopes of triggering *something*. When I did my initial digs on Phuc thirty-odd years ago and then, again, after the Ravensclere incident, only the barest memories threatened to flicker.

After hours, I thiiiiiink I managed to recollect an interaction or two with him from those days – almost hazily; the clearest was on the slopes of Pelion, at Kheirôn's home, that wisest of Centaur's school. I had journeyed there in the pique of my infatuation with Glaukos in search of answers – neither pity, nor hope was given me by Kheirôn or his pupils and I left in a dudgeon.

An adolescent Nomios, a young faun of somber moods and warm smiles despite my sharp words; a calm, contemplative Puca of mahogany skin and darker hair (he favors his mother, the nymph Penelopeia) who preferred the quiet company of a flock to the boisterous halls of man or faery. He smiled at me, as I left, golden lightning and brazen thunder wound about me, and seemed the closest to pity for my pain and heartsick anguish. As the younger son of Pan, he was one of the many Fae housed with mortal sons of kings and demigods of mythic propensity before he left and made his own way.

Our paths crossed a few times over the centuries before The War, nothing special that I can recall (although, once in southeastern Boeotia near a temple to the Charites, we danced at a godling's wedding) before he completely fell off my radar. Even after meeting him again and his pointed question – guaranteed to gain my attention – that night at Ravensclere as 'DJ Phuc', I only haphazardly managed to connect the somber, compassionate young Fae with the solemn Puca at Miss Nomer's side.

"The past is often something we tend to let lie behind us," the moon-cold silver Fae's voice is more subdued than a moment ago, drawing me back, as he leans against the wall; even half-hunched, he still towers over the painted silhouettes. "Although, speaking of the past and Nomios, I should apologize on his behalf – the … conversation last night veered into muddied memories that he does his best not to dredge up."

"He owes no one an apology," Tam's smile is genuine. "His grief and pain were clearly writ on his face; in his body language. If any forgiveness is to be meted out, it should be us asking it for causing him the pain."

That boy is smooth to a fault – but, he isn't wrong, either; so, I make a mental note to apologize in-person as soon as this case permits.

"Then, consider neither side in the wrong – nothing to forgive; nothing to forget; nothing owed," his mercurial eyes, half-hidden by the shades, glimmer as I place my hand on his shoulder. "Though, technically, I still owe you thanks for sending us to the Mourae – their alliance is the sort of footing this fledgling Court needs."

"It was my pleasure – I'm glad that you could help them."

And I really am; it frustrated me to no end that, *officially* we could do nothing until the proper channels were secured. Thankfully, Mabh gave my plan Her blessing. The literal and figurative reaching out between the Selighe Court and Court of Blood and Glitter has a bright, potential future ahead for Carterburg, its mortal and Fae denizens.

"Excuse me – Detectives Invidiosa and Linn? Sir?"

The young officer is back, smiling and standing behind the grey plinth displaying a krater and two small cups (of questionable quality), awaiting our attention.

"Hrmm – oh. Hello officer," I surreptitiously read his name badge, "Noble."

"That's right ma'am, George Noble; I'm sorry to say, Captain Walsh looks like he'll be indisposed for the rest of the afternoon – he asked me to convey his apologies."

Sharing a look, we're all quite sure he didn't even pretend to extend them.

"That's too bad – we were supposed to review the footage from the robbery with him," I answer, already thinking of ways to magically tap into the feed.

"That's why he sent me – I'm to escort you to one of our duty stations and review the footage with you there."

This kid – he's twenty-one, twenty-two at most, so … definitely a kid – may be overstepping his role, but, I'll take a polite kid trying too hard over an asshat officer impeding me any day.

Inside the cramped room, the whirr of overheated electronics and the air filtration system practically deafening, he pulls up the footage from the incident.

We watch, in a grainy mix of night-vision and black-and-white footage – multiple cameras' footage spliced together, as the shadows from either side of the display seem to congeal and form the striding shape of a boggle – gorgeous and skull-headed – and two Menacing Hobs. In a heartbeat, she's smashed the Lucite protective case and grabbed the gem from its display and, were the guards' not immediately nearby, she would have been able to melt back into the shadows with only the footage to prove her arrival.

Instead, they arrive and open fire – the first fires off a pair of shots (which either miss or pass harmlessly through the boggle) before the nearer Menacing Hob lifts him up and tears him in half. While the first guard is dying, the second and third continue their firing – the further one managing to hit one of the Menacing Hobs before being slammed across the floor and out onto the balcony. The middle guard, alone and covered in blood just … suddenly stops firing.

The boggle, her arm outstretched and leading with the gem, approaches him – made all the more eerie for the video's silence.

In a blinding flash of white light, the guard disappeared; standing stock still one moment, and gone the next.

"As you can see, the thieves stole exactly what they wanted and, after *that*," Officer Noble gestures at the carnage on the screen, "just disappeared."

He's right, as soon as they secured the gem, the trio just melted back into the shadows.

"Any chance you could zoom in on them and clean up the footage," Tam leans over Noble's shoulder and taps at the screen."

"Sadly, this is about as cleaned up as it gets; the computer automatically time-matched the various cameras' feeds – we're high-tech, but, not quite as well-off as film or TV would pretend. I can zoom in a little more on them, and pause shots is about it; just tell me which and where?""

He may be working here to pay for college – Anthropology major – but, the sheer kindness and believability in this kid? He could work wonders in politics.

"That spot – the boggle's face as she smashed the case."

"Too bad a charm to read lips wouldn't work here – no lips to read," Blodeuwedd's dry tone belies his frustration, and matches my own. It's true – between the bare skull of the boggle and the lip-less grins of the Menacing Hobs, there's nothing to even haphazardly guess at.

Pulling out the tablet, I snap a relatively clear photo of the boggle and send it to Taliesin.

"Is there a chance you could send a copy of this chunk of video to the Court of Faerie?"

"I mean, ermm, I think so?"

"Or, if not, could I?"

"I mean, if you happened to sit here," he offers me the chair, standing, "and >happened< to use a USB cord to transfer the open file from >this< port to your tablet … while I have my back turned, here," he turns, smiling to Tam and Blodeuwedd, "talking with your associates … how was I to know?"

Oh gods, I like this kid – I hope he doesn't get into any trouble for doing this.

"Thanks, Officer George Noble. Listen," I slip the USB cord and tablet back into my Hermes pocket – its unending depths are a constant blessing. "If you decide that this isn't the best route of paying your student loans, for whatever reason, the High Court of Faerie – especially its Royal Court Investigator (i.e. me) – is happy to aid. Mortals who take on in faerie service are well-compensated."

"I'll remember that, thank you ma'am."

As I gather the space between spaces about us, pulling Tam and Blodeuwedd with me into the aether, I laugh.

"Please, just call me Circe."

I enjoy the look of amazement on his face as we disappear.

7

FLASHBACK – two nights ago

The museum's corridors and entwining rooms were well-lit and clean; their emptiness the only betrayal of the late hour.

Throughout the building niches and cabinets were entombed behind Plexiglas and sliding doors, ready to be unearthed in the morning. Hallways and floors were patrolled by a handful of men in uniform; radios and flashlights at hand.

In the Gem Hall, behind bullet-proof glass, a chest-high pedestal was bathed in light by parallel bulbs whose twin shadows began to waver. The thick, undulating plinths of blackness began to trickle backwards like water pouring downhill over rock.

The pair of shadows crept and danced along the wall, skittering upwards and away from the light; they yawned and stretched like great cats. From their abyssal darkness, three shapes swiftly emerged; two great, mal-formed shapes in the rightmost one and a thin, comely one in the left.

All three were monstrous and terrible.

The blackness they stepped forth from clung to the leftmost one as if gauzy robing; its lustrously dark folds undulating in the still air while the perverted shapes of the Menacing Hobs, their elongated skulls and eyeless faces twisting in the stillness, maneuvered about the other in deference. The rank odor of the grave clung to their clammy skin.

Tall and lithe, her sun-darkened skin and long arms were adorned by works of gold, lapis, and copper. Each finger had two thin bands of braided red-gold encircling the foremost knuckle and, tonight, each ended in taloned, inky blades. Her dress was now formed of shadows that draped themselves about her. Its shape was cinched by a belt of woven gold and bone just below her bosom, which in turn, was covered by a great collar; its complicated pattern of bead, gem, and golden thread caught the light and sent it spinning.

Between strands of hair which snaked about in oil sleek beauty, a naked jackal's skull stared impassively at the gem's display – neither approving nor disapproving. Above her, as if a crown, a pale flame of corpse-white light hovered, its edges blurred and feathery. Two raven's wings danced where her ears might have been, twitching at the sounds of the mortal guards. All about her the scent of burning bronze and old, old blood dried on stone seeped into the air.

Before them, behind manmade defenses and deterrents, sat the London-Stuart Egg; its beautiful edges suffused with starlight and pristine swirls of diamond and silvery gold.

In an elegant, fluid movement the boggle smashed the "impenetrable" glass and snatched the Eye of Ma'at from its cushion; her motion completely unhindered by the museum's defenses.

"Sister," Imentet's voice was hollow, a broken eggshell of its former tenor; disembodied and ethereal. "Beware, there are innocents at hand."

Anupet, her attention divided, barely registered the arrival of the guards – the first was already dead, a sickly puddle of blood and broken bone, before she'd turned her eyeless face towards them. Behind his strewn twain parts, the second and third guards continued their firing; the furthest one managing to bury two bullets in the shoulder of the Menacing Hob to her right, the smell of its noxious ichor almost brought a retch to her throat, before he too disappeared – tossed away.

Stepping towards the ruckus, her bare feet made no sound on the marble floor as she approached the last, remaining guard. He made no move to flee or fire. Despite herself, she felt the magick slipping from her mouth. Thick words of power hung on the air – *Cease. Hold. Wait.* – the Glamour of Command lay in each and he stood, frightened and unblinking, at her approach.

The jewel, muddied by filigree and excess frippery, still burned brightly in her hand.

Beneath its trappings, the diamond throbbed in her grasp; glowing steadily, blindingly, brilliantly white. The Eye of Ma'at.

"Mesneh," she intoned. *Turn Backwards*.

A hollow rumble answered her.

"A'nen," she commanded. *Bring Back*.

Anupet couldn't have stopped it if she'd wanted to, and at this moment she wasn't sure she did, for the gem seemed possessed of a dire will of its own; tugging her arm heavenward. From her outstretched hand the diamond erupted in a heavy white light, bathing the guard in its brilliant corona.

And in the space between heartbeats, he disappeared.

"Sister," Imentet's tone was grey in her reproach.

"Spare me, I know that which I do," she lied. Certainty and determination, the last shoals she could grasp in the inundation of history and madness, would carry her.

"I see your heart," the worry colored her sister's voice, "and I know the feather of truth you weigh against it. You, like I, of all Fae know the roles of the barriers; the dead are dead and the living are to be pitied but, above all, they are to be loved. I tell you now, Anupet, I pity you and I do so love you. Senet, *sister*, do /NOT/ do this."

Smiling, such as her fleshless face could, she stared at the emptiness where Imentet hovered; unseen and heard only by her own guilty conscience.

Between the here-and-now and the there-and-then she flitted; the rich colors of her robe and beaded collar merely misty memories as they sat beneath her long black hair. Before, it fell – plaited and woven with Electrum and gold – nearly to her feet. If Anupet focused, she could almost make out Imentet's lovely, angular features, that of a Kite – that royal falcon – her golden eyes imploring and worried; her once-lustrous feathers now careworn and shabby.

"Alas, best-beloved sister of my heart, I must."

How long, she wondered, had it been since she'd seen their sisters, her daughter or husband?

Three thousand years? Or was it four.

She'd lost track of the passing ages in her unwilling service to the Mad Queene.

"Sister, your choice will end in madness if it fails, and worse-than-madness if it succeeds."

Silently, Anupet winced.

Near the end of The War when Angroboda, in her rage, had pillaged their temple in Southern Kemet, the sisters had feared for their lives. In a great house of limestone and marble on the Western bank of the river, a half-day's journey from the Nile's delta, they had lived serving the Kemetan people for many ages of man; worshipped and beloved.

"Dearest heart," Anupet whispered, "I fear I'm long-since mad."

Pulled from the bloodied mountain of slain mortals, they learned to live in abject and constant fear.

When their usefulness as tortured prey by Nemedh and his folk had ended, they were holed up in the dankest, darkest cell and left to rot; their only companions the muddy dirt they fashioned into likenesses of their family.

She missed her husband's crooked smile.

She missed their daughter's laugh which sounded like running water.

Anupet cursed the Fates – those heartless and needlessly cruel bitches – for the day when their crude manikins were discovered and Angroboda found a use for their waning magicks. And she cursed them nine-times-nine times for the day when the toll on Imentet was too much and Angroboda found a use for her dead body.

The shadows welcomed her into their cold embrace, their icy darkness clawing at her flesh, as the trio melted back into the spaces-between.

8

"Do you mind if I borrow your WiFi?"

We've just appeared in the private offices of *The Crossroads*, specifically Blodeuwedd's well-appointed chambers, and I'm eager to send the whole file to The Hollow Hill. While I'm not certain beyond a shadow on figuring out who, what, and how this all has happened, I have my guesses.

"Be my guest – the password is *GR13F*, all caps."

Leaning back into the leather armchair, I tap a brief message to Taliesin alongside the video before sending it to him. His answer is immediate.

'Got it. Will update you ASAP.'

His texts are seldom as verbose as he tends to be in-person – which, I've yet to decide if I find a blessing or vexing.

"That was … probably the most entertaining afternoon I've had in a very, very long time, Enchantress – Tamlinn. Thank you."

Behind his desk, Blodeuwedd has dropped the frippery façade of earlier in its entirety, his tone bordering on the formal familiarity I'm more used to as he shucks the coat and tosses it over the chair back. Stripping down to a low-cut and tight-fitting black t-shirt, he turns his back to us.

"Our pleasure," I flick Tam's shoulder – he's staring.

"I was thinking," Blodeuwedd regains my attention as he comes around to our side of the desk, toeing new boots on and zipping black jeans closed … that I don't know how we missed him changing into. "Seeing the boggle in-person, so to say, seems to have jarred something loose in my memories; something that's been flickering like broken starlight just out of the corner of my eye. Something about the London-Stuart Egg," he traced his long fingers across a dozen aged books, spine-out; their gilt titles and leather covers gorgeous.

"Ahh! This one," he pulls an especially thick tome from the shelf and plops it down on his desk with a decided thump; the weight of the book is impressive, six or seven hundred pages at least.

Skimming through passages over his shoulder, I recognize more than a few names and places within Faerie's northern realms; far countries of Faerie firmly within Angroboda's ruling. As he flips past a map, hand drawn and old, I see several familiar names, places I've never traveled to – like Élivágor of the Library, The Ironwood Forest, and Meidhmæris – for fear of Angroboda's untempered reach.

"I knew I'd remember it," Blodeuwedd turns the book out, splaying its pages for both Tam and me to read.

"The Eye of Ma'at," I read aloud, his fingertip poised above the description of the jewel for me, "A most precious of gemstones – ancient in its origins and beloved by Faerie and Man alike. Found within the red lands of Set by Wepset – "She Who Burns" – a daughter of Ra, and guarded by the sisters Anupet and Imentet; the gem burns with a holy white brilliance. The light, pure and unflinching, is considered to be the divine judgment/sight of Ma'at – goddess of truth, divine balance, order, harmony, and justice and most-sacred to Mother Cybele."

I mean, this does sound like the gem – how that boggle flashed a blinding white light at the guard right before he disappeared; it also fits with the boggle's overall rather Egyptian look.

"It goes further," Blodeuwedd turned the page where a drawing of a temple wall, complete with hieratic scale and Hieroglyphic nature, showed a woman holding the stone forth while rays emanated from it, bathing the prostrate man in front of her.

"Okay, I'll bite – this could be a great match; it fits the particulars and most of the evidence at hand. The only problem is, why hasn't this deathly ray of disappearance occurred before?"

"The Eye of Ma'at wasn't just an ornamental stone always 'on', Enchantress," Blodeuwedd leaned back against the bookshelf, his tone dancing between amusement and educator.

"Normal light shining through it, cool – brilliant and lovely and all that rot; but, when you commanded it, through words of power, the light was more. It was a bridge between the realms; a holy forefather of Faerie's Bifröst Bridge or the rainbow'd veils between the realms. Ma'at's role in the soul's judgment – her feather of truth, a good life lived – was a direct connection, by way of the stone's light, to the veils between the realms of the living and the dead. In the waning days of The Great War, when Angroboda and Nemedh," the hatred in his voice at their names would alarm me if I weren't already familiar with the long-standing enmity, "claimed the Eye of Ma'at (and many innocent Egyptian Fae as prisoners) after they sacked the temples, I'm assuming this was one of the plundered treasures."

I wince, recalling the sheer magnitude of destruction Faerie-on-Faerie war had brought to the world of man.

"I don't quite know what its journey was between the sacking of Faerie-held mortal lands and its placement within the Angroboda's Temple of Cybele in Meidhmæris, but … I'm assuming it was one of many relics of Faeries-on-Earth transposed to the Unselighe realm in those days. Whatever its journey, it resurfaced around the 9th century CE when the courtier, Lon Robbyn – i.e. a complete shitstain who still did his best to suck up to Angroboda after his city's fall from favor – plundered the disgraced temple's coffers and treasure houses (ostensibly in the name of the Queene. Of course, he kept the jewel back, holding it for himself in his grubby, greedy hands.)"

I'm intrigued. For all of the centuries of diplomacy Angroboda and Mabh have danced across the realms of Faerie, so much of what occurred within *Her* lands has remained ... *elusive*. Getting this little tidbit merely wets my curiosity.

Also – Lon Robbyn and Robhwyn London ... I wonder if there's more to that than casual nominal similarities. [*Note to self: look this up*]

"Our mutual friend that Nomios spoke of last night – the Fae who bartered the gem to the Stuarts for his rent? – told the story of its theft from Lon Robbyn once, deep in his cups, a few months after his arrival; no one believed him."

"Well, doesn't that just bugger all," Tam – quiet this whole time – is as shocked as I am. "And, of course, since the London-Stuart Egg is the selfsame jewel that explains why the boggle attacked Ciaran and the painting; tracking it down and using his own research against him."

"You're not just another pretty face, Blue."

"The real questions are: who is this boggle and why now?"

The opening strains of Mendelssohn's *A Midsummer Night's Dream* begin, interrupting, and I reach across the desk for my damnable phone, wincing to them both in apology. Turning it over, my nerves flutter in trepidation, before answering, "Hello".

"Circe, two things – good job at The Smithsonian, thank you; we're near to identifying the boggle and … will you *hold on*?"

I feel the insistent tug of a powerful spell, wending about my hand – the one holding the phone – and manage to pop out a surprised "Oh!" to Tam and Blodeuwedd at my side before the sensation of dislocation consumes me.

The lights shudder and blink out before a flash reveals the world anew.

"What in the bluddy name of fuckall Phlegethon was that about?!" I sharply yell across the icy bracken. Their hands on my elbows, Tam and Blodeuwedd stand – wobbily – by my side, tugged along with me to wherever here is.

"Apologies, Detective – but, this seemed the more expedient measure."

Standing on a large outcropping of granite looking down at me – at us – with a look somewhere between bemusement and amusement stands a Fae with bright, sea-cerulean eyes; his long blue-black hair is braided loosely over his right shoulder, while sandy linens and summer's golden robes shimmer in the chill breeze. Taliesin Kyanokhaitēs – "Blue-Dark Haired" in Attic Greek – and Taliesin Ben Beirdd – "Chief of Bards" in Middle Welsh. The Royal Consort, Prophetic Bard of the Nine Realms, Selkie Warchief, High Counselor of the Queene's Privy Council, and Official Court Spymaster.

In other words, my boss.

"'Expedient' my furry ass; really Taliesin."

"Which would you have preferred – a prolonged conversation via text or phone where *prying eyes*," he carefully enunciates, arching his brow behind me, "or a quick'n'dirty dispatch. I've always assumed, Detective, you prefer the latter."

The way he says 'Detective' brings to mind the mortal actors David Warner and Tim Curry; something about his precise annunciation on its dental plotives: dee-tEck-tiffv.

"Regardless, Circe, Tamlinn – I brought *you* here for a reason," again, his emphasis has me looking over my shoulder at Blodeuwedd (who looks less than concerned, nor amused).

"After your reports on Ciaran's missing Stuart Family files, I had Aneirin do his own cursory research yesterday … which brought up this idyllic little rock," he spreads his elegant hands to encompass the whole of the island. "Apparently, the Stuarts once owned it before it fell through *rather questionable* paths into the City's hands, who – in turn – placed it in private trust with The Friends of The River. When Aneirin was unable to contact the Laucks Island groundsman, a Ross Guerber, he popped over and, upon his findings, suggested I do the same. Now, I requested it of you."

Around us, I take in the sight of twisted, twining maple, birch and pine and rocky bracken falling towards the river on one side, a sandy beach is just visible through the brown and evergreen verge.

Silently, Taliesin drops down beside us, and we follow (begrudgingly, if I can guess at Blodeuwedd's mood) – stepping on a winding sandy path towards the wider end of the island.

"Taliesin, look," I whisper, catching up to the Bard. "Blodeuwedd reached out for me, *in concern might I add*, just the same as Tamlinn did – he's not the enemy."

"No," his voice is low but neutral. "He is not, although as of yet, he is not a *friend*; only time and The Fates will share that which lies ahead."

Perfect bardic enigmatic bollocks, *sigh*; why am I not surprised?

"You still haven't told me," I pull the frustration from my voice as we round a bend, "exactly *why* Mabh had Ciaran looking into the Stuart family."

Taliesin's pointed stare, off and to the left, is more frustrating than dry panattone (and twice as disappointing).

"Perhaps, you might help shed some light on these?"

Taliesin, stopping, resumes his formal tone and stands in a small clearing lightly dusted in half-hearted snow; the only growth old lichen over rock and decomposing leaves. At its center, between two deep holes, is a corpse – whom I'm assuming is the missing groundsman. The holes look incredibly deep; using a small will-o'-the-wisp I lean over and cast a golden green glow down the closest pit, gauging it to be at least twenty feet down.

Whatever was down there had a Sisyphean effort coming back up.

"While this is before my time, Taliesin ap Elffin," Blodeuwedd's voice is nearly melodic as he curtly bows, wrapping his Northern tongue around the Welsh and addressing this disarmingly dangerous Fae. Taliesin's right brow is raised in a mix of amusement and curiosity as he smiles, encouraging Blodeuwedd to continue.

(I've never thought of it, but, despite Blodeuwedd's Welsh name, there isn't anything else that reminds me of Cymru. His nearly-neutral – albeit rather posh – accent contains only clipped hints of Northern Ireland, mayhap The Shetlands, or even the Orcadian Norse-influenced Scots. And, once again, I'm struck by the fact that there is really so much I *don't actually know* about him.)

"But my guess is that these," he gestures at the deep pits yawning beside the corpse and grimaces, "were, until rather recently, graves for unnumbered Fae. You will find no record or mentioning of these deaths or their unmarked nature for the Stuarts had no wish to reveal their … *imperfect* past to any, let alone while negotiating with the Selighe Court."

Behind his casual remarks I hear the steel in his voice – I can see the diamond-sharp edge to Blodeuwedd's gaze.

"And what, Cybele tell, about the corpse laying here – exsanguinated?"

"My guess," Tam stands next to Blodeuwedd, his hand on the taller Fae's shoulder, "is that the selfsame boggle – aware of these deaths – exhumed the graves and murdered this man. The wintry chill would stay decomposition and scent; have you called the Carterburg Medical Examiner's Office yet – have they given a time of death?"

"Not yet, I had planned on doing so after our *chat*."

"I thiiiiiiiiiink," Tam turns to me and then back to Taliesin, "that our timeline is a bit jumbled; only making sense if you piece it back together like a broken mirror – connecting the largest pieces first."

Stepping around us, he continues, "If you follow me … this death is actually our starting point – well, inasmuch as it can be, occurring roughly five nights ago. While immaculately laid, it isn't 'fresh'; the cold isn't the only thing at work here – can you smell the preservative Glamour about his body? It reminds me of camphor and spider webs. I think that, either before or after pulling open these graves, the boggle murdered the groundsman – bleeding him dry; from there she attacked Ciaran while he was at his research into the

Stuarts (already aware of their connection to Laucks Island) before she eventually broke into The Smithsonian for the jewel. The Stuart family and its history is the only connecting point between all three."

"The Eye of Ma'at," I add. "From our research on its provenance, the Stuarts received the gem – once in the possession of a Northern Realms temple to Cybele – as payment for rent before converting it into the London-Stuart Egg for Lucy Stuart."

I can feel Blodeuwedd's hand on my elbow in-thanks for my discretion. That I've omitted the precise details Blodeuwedd and Nomios gave us is no concern to Taliesin – at least not yet, I hope.

"Then, that would explain the events to the northwest less than an hour ago."

His face tight, Taliesin sits down on the largest rock beside us, gesturing his acquiescence to our pieces and Tamlinn's explanation.

"Aneirin messaged me a few minutes before I summoned you – the boggle was seen approaching the outpost of Ofn Mynydd in Fauquier – near Goldvein and Summerduck, according to the Peredurdr shortly before all contact was lost. Ofn Mynydd was built to house the Glain Neidr – the great Seeing Stone – on an island similar to this," Taliesin's voice drops – almost as cool as the air about us and his gaze narrows. "Converted from a mill and smithy once owned by the Stuart family."

I can feel the Glamour shaping my bones into my preferred feline form before I even hear the order to go.

9

Soft, olive-toned flesh makes way for sleek amber and ginger-y golden fur as fingers make way for paws and my black hair sparkles into a thick rough of shimmering brightness; haloing me. In the blink of an immortal eye I'm back in Sidhe Cat shape, claw and fang ready for a fight.

The air shimmers as I tug the three of us into the spaces-between, and – after several long moments – aim for a spit of land, a promontory, with a wide view of Ofn Mynydd. The outpost, a great hillock of grey-green rock humped skywards, stands on a small island within Hedgeman's river.

The structure, with rough-hewn steps and windows circling about it, occupies the whole of the rock that rises from the waters. Its 'entrance', a great arch barred by iron and wood almost halfway up, sits above vast, dead roots and twining bare trunks that clamber at its feet; beneath the southernmost edge I can just make out the original mortal-cut stonework.

The whole is forbidding, grim and stern as it sits as bulwark between the edge of Faerie-influenced lands within Virginia and the wide world of Man beyond.

It's named Ofn Mynydd, *Pointe Dread*, for a reason.

"Yaldi! Ullaich màthairfuckers," beside me, Tam's slipped into near-undecipherable Scots as he tosses his coat on a nearby branch – dislodging snow and suddenly wielding two large daggers I didn't know he had on him. And behind me, brandishing a sword of silver and sapphire – seriously, where are those two pulling these weapons – is Blodeuwedd, grim and silently determined.

"A frontal assault or sneak in?" Tamlinn grimaces, staring off.

"If I were this boggle – I do so wonder who she is, or was – I'd assume that stealth would be the likeliest course and prepare for it."

"What if we give her both, Enchantress?"

Turning, I cock an ear to Blodeuwedd, intrigued by his line of thinking.

"You and Little Boy Blue are the heavy hitters here – not to downplay my own skills – and are the likeliest to be expected; if you make a brash and direct attack – blades, claw and magicks flying, she'll throw the majority of her forces to counter you. While I, in shadowy Glamours, sneak in through that window," his glistening black nail indicating a eastward-facing window.

"Why that one?" beside us, Tamlinn's concern is telltale.

"Because the main door is almost western-facing for one reason," Blodeuwedd points out.

"And for another," I add, "obviously the boggle is Egyptian, from her garb and jackal's skull as well as her knowledge of how to use (and determination to possess) the Eye of Ma'at – correct? And any schoolgirl – or schoolboy – in the lands of Faerie or Midgard even haphazardly learned in their culture knows the West to be sacred and the pathway to the lands of the dead. If this boggle is after a great Seeing Stone and already has a gem that can pierce the veils between the 'Lands of Death and Life' it stands to reason that she'd be working facing West and more vulnerable to an eastern intrusion."

"Stealth and brute force – a winning combination."

I can't fault Blodeuwedd's reasoning.

"So, we draw the cannon fodder, you slip in and … what? Steal the gem and stick a blade between her ribs?"

"Something like that, Enchantress – trust me."

But can I trust him?

I *want* to trust him.

"Okay – Tam, follow me; Blodeuwedd wait until you see them swarming and then make your move. Got it?"

Blodeuwedd, the sword glinting in his hands, nods.

"Seadh," Tam mutters, his blue eyes almost grey in this light.

Wrapping my tail about Tam, I glide us – invisible and insubstantial – down from the ledge and across the airs, landing with a nearly silent 'thud' on the moss-slick stone. Thankfully, it seems that the warmth of the rushing river keeps the ice at bay.

Up close, the arch and draw-door are rather daunting in their archaic fashion. In a breath, I drop the Glamour and throw the magickal equivalent of a thunderclap against the walls. Bright, summer's golden light hammers at the rock and searches against every crack, nook and crevice for purchase; shaking the stones and clawing at the mortar.

If I have to, I'll bring the damn place down about us to get their attention.

Thankfully, it doesn't seem that I have to go that far, as Menacing Hobs – far more of them than we'd guessed were at her disposal – come pouring out of the tower windows; crawling down the rock like grey, ashen spiders.

The draw-door slams against the stone doorstep with an answering thunderclap at my paws as a pair of Nubs, eleven feet tall and their grotesquely equine features contorted in pain and hate, shoulder through the shadowy archway. Behind them, its features hidden by shadow, a Southern Ettin grins – its tusks and razor-filed teeth gleaming in the half-light of the tower.

"I'll take the ugly fucks on the left, you take the ugly fucks on the right," Tam's laugh as he launches himself at the closest Nub is madcap; he's been learning the absolute worst lessons from me … and it makes me love him all the more.

Throwing myself at the second Nub, I cast sprite-fyres at the swarming Menacing Hobs; engulfing their twisted forms in electric green and blue flames and filling the air with the stench of burning, putrid flesh. I'd try traditional routes – tooth and claw and brute force, but their numbers are more than troubling – alone, they'd be a task unto themselves. Add to that the fact that the Nub is wicked fast for its size, it's taking more of my concentration and effort to remain out of its maw than I'd like to admit.

An old saying whispers behind my eyes, 'Damn the beast all 'round the week – through to Sunday and back.'

Four arms, each ending in thick-fingered hands, grasp and crush the air … where I've just been. Ddancing in a wickedly wild pattern, I'm keeping two steps ahead of this behemoth; but, it isn't easy. His eyes, all six, are flaming red and watching me – judging my jumps, strikes and pounces. His long, tapered jaw seems to wrinkle in pleasure as he swats with one left hand and I dodge, badly, directly into the lesser right hand.

Metrokoites.

His grip is ridiculously strong – I can feel ribs threatening to crack. I have seconds to act before he'll eat me, shoving me down his tooth-filled gullet; a most ignominious death I have absolutely no interest in.

Before I succumb to the pain, I bite down on the soft flesh between thumb and forefinger; my mouth filling with vile blood and rabbit kick my hind legs into his palm, gouging through meat and bone.

With effort (and more than a little luck), I mix magicks with blood and in a (pained) heartbeat, golden-green liquid light begins pouring from my mouth; flaming amazement about us and into the archway at the Nub's back.

I cry "Havoc!" and let slip the 'cats of war' – caustic flames wreath my whiskers and surround his face, pouring down his throat and ripping into him. Sprite-fyre cats, each mimicking me as they fill him, surround him, and fry him from both the inside out and outside in.

Not a trick I recommend, unless you enjoy the sensation – and lingering aftertaste – of charbroiled Nub, vinegary blood, and stomach acid.

It's also bluddy exhausting.

Beside me, on the curving steps, I see Tam dispatching the other Nub – limbless and now headless – into the flowing waters.

From behind me a low, guttural laugh ripples along the lingering flames as the Southern Ettin steps into view.

Taller than a Nub, but shorter than his Northern brethren, the Ettin's features would be handsome – high cheekbones, long black hair, sunbaked skin – were it not for the twisted aspects of tusk and fang.

"Go, 'Cee – I got this," Tam turns from me, smiling, and towards the approaching Ettin; his daggers slick with blood and a halo of electric blue flames behind him. "Bàsachadh mu thràth," I hear him mutter as he runs towards the threat and I leap upwards, towards the open southern window.

I hope that the Ettin will just 'die already', too,

Landing, my paws slick with sweat and blood, I find myself in a great, circular chamber – the high walls bare, save for the imprecise and irregular lines of stone while Bronze Age sculptural art and hammered Ogham script delineate the areas within. A large stairwell, flanked by braziers of copper and gold, fills the far wall. Around the room are littered the bodies of the Peredurdr's attendants, their weapons and innards strewn about. At its center, on a raised dais, is a glowing chunk of granite – a great round hole its sole feature; aside from the corpses, I'm alone.

Guttural, warped whispers suddenly echo around the chamber's high walls as I pad about, sniffing and I slip behind the central dais, a plinth nearly twice my feline height, and wait.

"Ibetj teftef haty-ek mehy," the boggle emerges from the stairwell's archway; her voice is raspy but lovely, like ancient jewels long left in the dry desert sun to bake, their edges sharpened by wind and sand. The braziers' flames and her own halo'd wisp cast her monstrous visage of bone and fang into flickering beauty. About her is an air of ancient, sacred magic; like a sharp heat haze that tastes of copper, lilies, and salt.

From my vantage point I can't see whom she's speaking to, nor do I hear a response; but, she pauses and leans back against the cold stone to answer the unseen.

"Sewered pu djed en-ek," her tone is weary as she holds an elegant hand at her bony temple, the flame above her dancing.

My ancient Ægyptian may be rusty, but I'm pretty sure that she just told whomever she's with that they're literally exhausting to talk with.

A (nearly) silent footfall behind me draws my attention to the slip of stone as it shifts beneath an image of Peredur – who stands victorious over the Addanc – where Blodeuwedd silently smiles, before winking at me as he pushes a hidden door closed behind him.

His sword, hanging from the studded black leather belt at his hip seems smaller, wieldier, before it shimmers from view while his left hand shoves something small and glistening into his pocket.

'Got it,' he mouths before gesturing for me to stay where I am.

"Aw ibetj," he calls out across the room, his voice strong and his tone commanding as he strides across the floor, passing me and drawing the boggle's attention to him like a lodestone. "*Greetings and may your heart rejoice,* She Who is in the Place of Embalming and Protectrix of the Dead."

Protectrix of the Dead?

Anubis is the god of embalming and protector of the-, oh.

Oh!

That means he's guessed her to be Anupet, Anubis' wife and one of the far-too-many Egyptian Fae who disappeared in the wake of The Great War. This makes absolute sense; if any faerie would have a connection and awareness of how to use the stone, it would be an attendant goddess of death and resurrection and one of the stone's original protectors!

"Greetings, Re'pat," her voice is cracked, her tone wry.

If a bare skull could make a snarky grin, methinks she would. But Re'pat ... *Prince?* Is she mocking him as the Queen of Blood and Glitter or is there more to it than that?

The flames dancing about her have a decidedly warmer hue than before as she tilts her head, the black feathery wings fanning themselves at odd angles like a bird amused and confident. I can't decide if she's listening to the unseen presence beside her or merely gauging Blodeuwedd's reaction (or lack thereof as he's barely moved, his face stony, waiting for her to continue).

"Do not be surprised, Ianew Sen'Ahew, that I know you despite yourself and despite myself. Of what use would I have been to Her were truths and lives, stories, deaths and names so easily sidestepped?"

If I read Blodeuwedd's stony silence correctly, she's touched a nerve. But which and why?

"The stories and the threads dance between worlds, between lives of the living and the dead, *Son of Grief*; so enmeshed and entwined that their truths are contradictory," her long, elegant hands sweep outwards to encompass the room and the great Glain Neidr behind which I crouch. "Histories ill-remembered and heart-griefs buried do not change what we were; what we are. Believe me Re'pat Ianew, I've tried. In my grief I cannot forget just as truly as I cannot remember," her voice is broken from pain and ... something else I can't quite put a paw on. Longing? Madness? Grief?

"When the webs we weave of grief and vengeance ensnare their quarry, those selfsame threads bind ourselves as inexorably as they bind our prey and together we leap into the fathomless."

I … I want to follow her here, but, I don't think I can; the metaphors, homilies, and similes are a bit much if not overly muddled.

"We need not be bound by *Her* or it, milady," Blodeuwedd's voice has lost all of its humor, he isn't playing for time so much as he's bracing for her next move.

She saunters across the floor, passing close enough I could cut her with a claw if I but reached out a paw – but Blodeuwedd's stern look curtails that – instead, I shift to the opposite side of the dais, silently staying in its shadow.

"Oh but not so - for history is not forgotten by the dead, even if it is forgotten by the living," the dark hollows where her eyes once were burn suddenly with a feverish, gallows-green glow, her voice and cadence are suddenly far more aggressive than the sing-song of a moment ago. Beside her, two of the slain faeries begin to stand like puppets whose strings are tangled.

"I am damned even as I try to find refuge, hope, and peace."

Whorls of grave-dust flit from her hands and dance about the pair, enveloping them in twin sandstorms. Their rich robes of cerulean and watercress shred in the onslaught, leaving behind thin strips of undyed linen to cover their chests, wrists, and groins. Their dead flesh, now sallow and grey, becomes gaunt and stretched tightly over thin, overly-elongated limbs as their skulls pull like taffy into contorted, unrecognizable shapes.

Except, I do recognize them.

"Ankh udja seneb!" *Life, strength, and health!*

As the whirlwinds dissipate, two Menacing Hobs stand now beside her, their grotesque forms eyeless and grinning, where the bodies of faerie priests lay just moments ago.

Fates blast Her; oh what the mad Queene has wrought – this gross parody of Anupet's role in the cycle of life and rebirth has Angroboda's black fingerprints all over it.

And suddenly the swarm of Menacing Hobs and two great pits of empty faerie graves on Laucks Island make sense; the only true mystery here is … why now? Why did Anupet make a move now? Why did she draw the connection between the Stuarts, the jewel, and the Selighe Court's own investigation right now?

"Anupet, *now* would be good time to discuss the ramifica-… oh fuck it – **NOW Enchantress! NOW!**" Blodeuwedd's voice holds none of its usual languor as he sprints across the room towards the boggle; the silver and sapphire sword suddenly back in his hands (I really must ask him how he does that).

I spring forward and bowl over the nearer of the Menacing Hobs, my claws neatly slicing its undead flesh and its spilling black blood. Gagging, I suppress an urge to look for any remnant of the faerie it was in its twisted features.

As I make literal mincemeat of the one, the other Menacing Hob has rushed Blodeuwedd; its long arms and deadly claws raking the space where he danced just out of its reach. With a grunt, he swings his blade and neatly decapitates the foe as silvery blue flames dance about its now twice-dead corpse.

Before I can warn him, though, Anupet has slapped him – appearing at his side and backhanding him – and snatched the glowing object from his pocket (what I'm assuming is the Eye of Ma'at that he'd neatly stolen from wherever she'd hidden it).

Another dozen of the eyeless monsters are sprinting towards us as they hustle up the stairwell from the vast depths of Ofn Mynydd's twining chambers.

It seems our hands are going to be full for a minute.

"You're acting like a mosquito after wolves."

Beyond us, her tone unamused, Anupet has turned away – no longer concerned with either of us – and is chanting as she embraces the Glain Neidr; intoning words of power and command in a dozen tongues of Man and Faerie. Runes of fire, ice, star, and bone dance in parti-colored light about us as an irresistible tide of magic erupts. Its energy pushes and pulls at us in an avalanche of magic.

At its zenith, in the eye of the storm, stands Anupet; calm and erect.

Like a long pent-up breath, an ancient force now thrums about us in bracketing waves, seeking to dislodge the whole world in its wake; fingers of glittering magic pick at the fibres of reality, worming between the warp and weft that bind it all together and quaking the entirety of Ofn Mynydd to its roots.

Shaken from the sheer power she's unleashed, it's all we can do to hold our own in combat with the horde of Menacing Hobs, cutting them down inelegantly and inefficiently as we slowly make our way back across the room towards her.

The air is thick with disastrous magic, filaments of ghastly light and color make it hard to see further than the nearest foe. But, as I strike down one of the last of the Menacing Hobs, I can see Anupet – her hand glowing from the burning Eye of Ma'at – as she plunges her outstretched arm into the center of the great Seeing Stone.

For a moment the world hiccoughs.

Colors are inverted, shadow and light bleed past each other, and taste and hearing seem to play at odds with one another.

The western-facing window, the one Blodeuwedd had mentioned earlier, is gone – the whole wall has been replaced with a flickering after-image.

The edges of it are both singed in blackened shadow and lapping like a lake of white light in a summer's breeze.

I have a headache just trying to focus on it.

"Sister, what have you done?"

Interlude

FLASHBACK – a few minutes ago

Two more Menacing Hobs fell; their foetid ichor staining Tamlinn's suede shoes a rank and putrid mess as they tumbled piecemeal into the flowing waters of the Hedgeman. 'Ugh,' he thought as an arc of electric blue flame washed over a third smoldering its flesh down to the bone, 'these are getting chucked in the dustbin as soon as I find one – I'd rather fight barefoot.'

Above him, he watched Circe gracefully land on the open windowsill and disappear within the shadowed recesses of Ofn Mynydd; while, in front of him, the Southern Ettin growled a deep and monstrous laugh.

Despite complete absurdity of their fight, he too laughed.

Other battles danced across his memory – slashes of crimson and faerie steel in field and courtyard, of moonless nights and sunless dawns. Across the whole of Faerie and against so, so many of Twilights Children he had fought – on behalf of his Queene and for himself.

Tamlinn.

Elf Knight.

The Queene's Blade.

He'd quarreled and dueled on behalf of honor and on behalf of love – no matter how many centuries had passed, he'd held fast to that; keeping friends at a distance with quips and snark for he never counted tomorrow as a given. Ever, his sword and daggers had been nigh unbeatable – whether fair combat or not, he'd acquitted himself well and reveled in the challenges and the battles he faced.

But he hadn't assumed tomorrow and tomorrow's tomorrow.

Not since his duel with Nemedh on the time-locked sandy shores of Ynys Tylwyth Dawnswyr had he felt the battle craze so nearly overwhelm him. The heady thrill of muscles crying out in exertion; the melody of his daggers as they bit through flesh and bone; the joy as fist and wit danced heedlessly against all comers; the song of battle was, as always, absolutely intoxicating. He almost relished the berserker madness and complete loss-of-self to it.

Almost.

The world-reeling pain, though, as the Ettin smacked him sideways with a bronze cudgel the size of a fridge, brought him up short and violently reminded him of reality.

Stars blackened around him and his vision swam; the world lurched violently as he stumbled, trying to regain his footing. Peril hovered like a cloud about his waning consciousness when, through it, a shimmering glow seemed to rush. It was a silvery shimmer, but, for some reason, it reminded him of Simon's emerald eyes.

Warm and welcoming.

Comforting and safe.

His wits returned to him in a rush.

He fumbled blindly for his daggers behind him as he lay sprawled, not daring to look away from his foe, but found nothing more than broken rock slick with blood and entrails.

Wincing, he realized belatedly that some of the blood was his.

'Wha'ever gods be blest, I promise – get me out of this scrape and I'll stop putting off dinner with Simon's mother; Hels, I'll even bring dessert.'

Through the pain, he watched as the Ettin got closer.

Flexing his left hand, he gripped the loose shale and granite about him and began flinging it like so much elfshot at the Ettin; igniting the blood with neon blue sprite-fyre and pelting the monster as it loomed closer. The behemoth would have shrugged it off, as unconcerned as if they were no more than gnats, if he hadn't almost stumbled on the shadowy slick rock. Swinging the cudgel, he planted its blunted end in a sharp crack and braced himself against it to face Tamlinn's barrage.

'Feck' Tamlinn frowned as he watched the monster as righting himself, suddenly surefooted. 'Merlin's balls, but Ettins' intelligence are woefully unsung. How in the nine hels am I supposed to do more than piss it off– eh? What's that?'

Beside him, in the afternoon's sun, a small shape shone glittering-white and red: a slip of a dagger – silver with a large cabochon garnet in its pommel – whose blade was half-buried in the rock.

'It must've been one of the priests',' he thought as he reached for it.

As his bloodied fingers wrapped around its handle, the blade flickered like glistening snow and grew in length – what had been a dagger was suddenly a lance-length sword of Nidavellir steel; lightweight and deadly beautiful.

"Just call me Arthur of the Brythons," he laughed as he rose.

Ignoring the pain in his ribs and back, he swung the deadly blade in earnest arcs at the Ettin he advanced. He sang as he watched his foe's smug assurance slip away; his handsome features marred by copious cuts as his brackish blood began to flow from the numerous wounds the Elf Knight dealt

. . . .

Landing invisible and shadow-light, Blodeuwedd snuck around the unnerving sight of a Menacing Hob as it guarded a large, stone door.

No matter his age, no matter how often he saw them, they still managed to twist his guts with their absolute unnatural wrongness. Their terrifying visage clawed at the fragmented memories of his life *before* – of his broken years in the shadows of his mother's monstrous Court.

Despite the threat of nausea – the bile was already slowly rippling at the back of his throat – he knelt behind the creature and tried to sense what was in the locked room that warranted guarding. A blinding flash of anguish, exquisite in its piercing beauty of iridescent white, confirmed his guess that the Eye of Ma'at lay sat beyond.

A simple un-binding curse silently aided his lock picks as he crouched, hardly breathing and praying to all of the dead gods he could remember that his Glamour kept him hidden; a soundless breath, held tight and finally released, accompanied the feathery feel of the locks giving way.

Between moments, he slipped through the doorway's crack and closed it behind him; adding his own binding curses to the door just in case the Menacing Hob got suddenly curious.

Turning from the door, he began to investigate the room – unremarkable in its generalness; the walls were the same stone of the keep, a lichen hued grey-green, while the room itself was semi-circular and filled with built-in shelves of a weathered umber-toned wood. Most of the shelves were filled with dark, unprepossessing boxes or thick, leather-bound tomes as they curved around the arc of the room. At the far point was one of the many windows that studded the outside of the forbidding edifice; it's pointed arch was braced by thin glass and broad stone a slightly greener shade – perhaps, he mused, brightened by the priests' palms as they looked out at the vista.

The view, as he leaned out the window, was breathtaking; from this height he could see vast stretches of woodland as it billowed outwards in twiggish browns and evergreens, broken by sporadic slithers of asphalt and small neighborhoods dotting the snowy fields in-between; while the Hedgeman's River flowed in leaps and gurgles from the hazy, violet-hued western mountains, off southwards, towards Carterburg and further east towards the Chesapeake.

He shivered at it all.

Memory pulled at him and for a brief moment he saw a similar vast plain; Nidavellir, stretching from the frigid mountains – whose jagged peaks tore at the sky – down towards the great Ironwood Forest.

Despite the magnificence before him, in the here-and-now, he quelled – the bucolic beauty and peace offered by the view tugged at his heart and, just as equally, repulsed him. Intellectually he knew that this sort of quiet was what he should want and yet …

And yet.

Irrevocably, he was bound to urban space – whether the labyrinthine corridors of power in his mother's obscene palace and its opulent city of Élivágor or Carterburg's mix of mortal and Fae, he would always be drawn to the spaces.

His heart hammered in dread at that soft peace.

And, suddenly, he wondered – how long had his emotions been so volatile? He picked at the stone chips beneath his nails as he worried; yes, they'd been rawer, closer to the surface since he'd entered Euphrosyne's wood. His temper, always mercurial, had been … more extreme in the days since. The concerns of Nomios and Johann and of Circe tugged at him in songs of pity and rhymes of terrible love.

Nifl-damned it, as they told the truth to her last night he could barely contain his grief and rage at what had happened.

Blodeuwedd the Miss Nomer was cold control.

If he didn't have that, what *did* he have?

A laugh, familiar and nearly manic in its tenor, caught Blodeuwedd's attention as he stood there nearly mesmerized by the tranquility and internal conflict; tugging him from his unwanted introspection

Below, on the "doorstep" – the wide ledge partly encircling Ofn Mynydd – he saw a Southern Ettin as it bore down on the elf knight. Tamlinn's laughter abruptly stopped as the monster threw him across the sharp and broken stone with his club; the twin-bright arcs of silver landing amidst the shoals told him that the faerie's daggers were out of reach.

"Oh you foolish hero – Little Boy Blue what can you do with no horn to blow?" he muttered, half to himself and half to the universe before he pulled a slim, silvery dagger from the crook of his boot and eyed the scene.

'I'm going to miss you, aren't I?' he half-sang as he held the blade. 'Go now!'

Yet another emotionally powerful reaction; he winced at himself as a crooked smile threatened to break past his defenses. This new emotional vulnerability would have to be dealt with … but later.

Flicking oilslick shards of rainbow at the Ettin's feet, he threw the dagger a handbreadth from Tamlinn's prone form before turning back to the room, (certain the knight would right himself and save the day) and resumed his hunt for the gem.

"Where oh where has my little gem gone – oh *where*, oh *where* can you be?" Blodeuwedd infused words of power into the fetching spell, half-closing his eyes as he waited.

A thin, watery buzz of accompanying pale light hummed in return, pulling him towards an engraved box of ebony covered in whorls of ivory and lapis; his gaze kept trying to slip off of it – pushed by the boggle's protective magic around the chest. A dozen interlaced spells of binding and containment held themselves around it, trying to hide the gem's glow and dissipate his summoning song.

'Every bait and switch is a work of art,' he thought to himself as he ruthlessly and effortlessly plucked at the frayed ends of spells and ragged edges of cantrips and curses like so much gift wrapped tape, leaving them in midair as he opened the box. Beneath the frosty glow, the Eye of Ma'at was beautiful as it sat on a cushion of silvery-blue satin and silk, even encumbered by the mortal propensity for over-ornamentalizing jewelry. Dropping a pebble the size of his thumb, he'd plucked it from the promontory while they planned, he wove a mild Glamour of Mesmer on it. In theory, he supposed, whoever opened it would be momentarily dazzled and bamboozled – a fallback if the Enchantress didn't stop the boggle in time.

Seamlessly, he patched the box's protections back together and left it where he'd found it.

He held the jewel in-hand and marveled at its feeling – it didn't sit cold like stone, it felt like glittering hope; warm and sharp at the same time. Memory, cold and cutting, warm and bittersweet, threatened again to overwhelm and distract him as he clutched it in his palm.

Slipping his sword back in-hand, he felt the jewel's tug slowly diminish.

'Now, I certainly can't go out the way I came in – I doubt I could mask both my presence AND cloak the stone's power right now; maybe there's another way out that doesn't require me literally climbing the walls,' he mused, blanching a little at the thought of inching along the sheer rock of Ofn Mynydd towards another window, clutching the sword and gem.

Turning, he slipped the sword back in the leather belt-loop on his hip and ran his hand along the bare wall that faced the window. Pushing his senses through the stone and mortar, he paused and concentrated; a soft click and susurrus of stone caused him to step back when a piece of wall swung into the room, revealing a hollow path barely tall enough for him to duck through. The space beyond was shadowed by a thick tapestry of heroic Peredur as he slew the great Addanc ... and beyond that?

Beneath the grand skylight at the center of the domed hall, behind the plinth where the 'seeing stone' sat, he saw Circe huddled – watching as the boggle slowly made her way into the room.

Heady waves of fizzing emotion and unstable power rippled across the room and, from the dozens of cuts and pooled blood he could see in her ginger fur, the enchantress was in no shape to tackle the boggle directly. Not yet.

Change of plans, then.

Winking, Blodeuwedd silently pushed back the tapestry and pulled the hidden door closed. Wrapping violet and jet Glamours of un-seeing about it, he tucked the gem into his jeans pocket and stepped slowly from the shadows.

10

Despite the unevenness of the world right now, and the throbbing headache the piercing light is giving me, the shape of a beautiful bird-headed faerie through the bright-white wall is clear.

And she is clearly concerned.

"Sister," Anupet's voice is firmer, less entangled than before as she pulls herself up from the ground; cradling the singed arm close to her breast. "Is that truly you?"

With a smile on her beak and blinked-back tears, she nods.

"Despite my admonishments, my fears, and worries, you did it. The veils are broken, Anupet – shredded like cloudstuff for the moment – death and life, afterdeath and the worlds beyond are no longer separate."

Beside me, the scattered Menacing Hobs corpses have begun to revert into the breathing forms of the Peredurdr and his priests, while a very alarmed pair of security guards appears – one with an odd slash midway through his uniform shirt. Behind them stands the groundsman, looking quite alive if not confused and further back are several very haggard and weary-looking Fae who stand apart, eyeing us as if unsure of who to trust.

Curioser and curioser: I'm just guessing here, but, I'd bet that they're the faerie-corpses Anupet exhumed from Laucks Island – probably the selfsame who helped her put together the Stuart puzzle.

Behind the bird-headed faerie several other shapes begin to coalesce; vague outlines coming into sharp relief – a tall, smiling jackal-headed faerie places his hand on the faerie woman's shoulder as a lioness-headed faerie and a smaller cobra-headed woman join them through the veil of white while a slight, wolf-headed man stands further back.

"Our whole family is here, Anupet," the jackal-headed man's voice – undoubtedly Anubis – is rich, a baritone born for songs of joy and revelation. "Repyt, Imentet, even little Kebhut; we have been waiting for you my love – my heart – for an age of ages."

Beneath his kind gaze, Anupet has shrunk – pulling her arms tightly about her, the raven's wings enfolding themselves about her bare skull. One hand is tugging at her long hanks of hair while the other picks at the threads of her skirt; silent tears running down the bone of her cheeks.

She doesn't need words to say that she's ashamed of what time and the tortures of Angroboda have done to her; what revenge and grief have wracked upon her – what she's survived and done. Everything about her now telegraphs it and I can't help it, despite the death she's dealt, my heart goes out to her.

"My wife," his hand and voice are firm as he lifts up her chin.

Where sharp angled and fleshless skull was but a moment before, velvety grey and black fur now ripple across her features. The sharp edges of bone and pain dull and curve as kohl-limned ferny-green eyes glow beneath long lashes.

Beneath the air of the room, I could swear I hear the beating of great wings between each moment.

"We chose our path between the stars and the earth, my love; behind the moon and beneath the sky beyond. To walk it together once more ... "

"I thought I'd lost you forever," her voice is barely a whisper.

"Never."

"I've done so many things, I did so, so-"

"I know," his voice is soothing on so many levels. I can hear the undying, unyielding, love in it and a (not so) little bit of me is jealous of Anupet for that. I've never been lucky in love.

"Imentet tried to stop me, but-"

"You had to do this your own way, sister; regardless of the risk and the dangers to the wide, wide worlds." Imentet's voice is soft as warm butter as she interrupts, "I should have been more understanding."

"I risked so many to do," Anupet clutches her breast, unable to finish.

"Hush. Look about you my heart, the balance is restored," he gestured towards the rapidly filling room about us. "When the balance was broken, I lost my love between the cracks of the world millennia ago," Anubis crooned, his long fingers grazing the newborn curves of her cheek; the ache in him for Anupet is almost beyond words – it's palpable. "Watching you in pain – unable to help you was an agony born of Set and more painful than the bite of Apophis," his voice is steel in velvet.

I can feel tears tumbling down my own furry cheeks.

"Whether you knew it or no, I have always been there – been here – for you. For ages in Angroboda's dungeons and the fractured shadows thereafter I reached out to catch the pieces as your world fell down and could only watch as you suffered – as I suffered. Unable to call you; unable to touch you; unable to comfort you. Wife – dearest part of my soul – I promise you that behind the veils or beside you, I have felt and known your love and hoped with every prayer that you felt mine."

"Anupet," Blodeuwedd calls from beside me as uses his sword as a makeshift crutch to approach – his leg bleeding freely, "you have to forgive yourself for *surviving* – for surviving *Her*."

"Forgive yourself," I add, my heart suddenly full to bursting. "Let your heart be the feather."

A great, keening sob of loss and joy erupt from Anupet and its power permeates all of reality as, with a haunting smile and beautiful laugh like the tinkling of crystal bells, she crushes the gem between her hands.

The rumble of its broken power colors creation for a moment.

The gem's magic had touched upon every branch of Yggdrasil, across realms and worlds-between-worlds I can only imagine; its loss is a thunderclap of unreality.

For a moment – or a hundred heartbeats – it feels like I can't breathe. Crushing pressure like Cetus kisses beneath the Aegean threatens to bury me.

And then, suddenly, it's over.

The tide has gone out and in its wake a peaceful air seems to settle about her and Anupet suddenly smiles – one of those smiles of pure, joyful relief and I can't help but notice how beautiful she is (you know, when not a skull-headed boggle murdering folk).

Laughing, free – truly free – she leans towards her husband's embrace.

And the universe goes uneven again.

11

Three nights later

The nearest I can figure is that when Anupet went
wherever it is that Anubis and their family were – whichever
realm behind the heavens it is – she pulled the veils closed
behind her and fixed everything after them. The effects of

whatever she did seem to be localized – both in physical proximity (Ofn Mynydd) and metaphysical (in regards to Anupet herself).

Thank the Fates.

I don't even want to think about what all would have been needed to clean up that giant turd-sandwich of a mess.

Earlier today Taliesin and I crafted a substitute London-Stuart Egg (using diamonds and other such mined in Faerie) to give the Smithsonian (who've extended their thanks – not from the still-absent Wolsh, but the Smithsonian itself); all of the dead priests and mortals are alive again – no harm, no foul there – and we even have a few new/old faeries to integrate into Carterburg society.

Happy Endings all around.

Things wrapped up nicely, didn't they?

Only … they didn't.

What's going to happen when these sudden-survivors of mortal hatred are exposed to the Carterburg of now? Tommy Brennan was right, in spite of the general pleasantry of the Fae District and baseline comfort of Carterburg itself, the growing dissent fueled by homophobic and feyphobic rhetoric has grown over the last few years. Or, worse, it's just feeling emboldened. The attacks on Anthony and Kenneth Hall after they left *The Crossroads* a year and a half ago was just the beginning [*note to self: get with the Carterburg DA about following up on these cases*] – numerous "good ole boy" moments of friction have risen – from suburban Stefford, through Hartwood and into Falmouth along the northeastern riverside of town. More of Carterburg's Stefford-side neighborhoods have … well, felt openly uninviting. Gentrified, and iron-shod. From Tam's reports, a fair bit of the energy going into that stems from the budding popularity of Carterburg's nascent Church of the Word [*note to self: work with outlier confidential informants and look into their inner practices*] – an incredibly popular non-denominational church just across the river.

Despite the potential danger, I doubt that we can convince them to remain in the Hollow Hill instead of returning to Carterburg; something tells me that the reasons for their émigré from Faerie, as Phuc mentioned, have not lessened in the short time they lived on earth and may be exacerbated by the current clime of official Faerie/mortal interaction. It's going to be a long few weeks ahead of constantly beating my head against a brick wall, isn't it?

sigh

As we were going through Anupet's effects – she didn't leave much behind – in the storeroom where the gem had been hidden, we found Ciaran's reports for Mabh (and by 'we' I mean Blodeuwedd and me as Tamlinn, Aneirin, and Taliesin were busy making sure the Nubs and Ettin were still quite dead and getting the Peredurdr and his priests all sorted). I took photos of the files before turning them over to Taliesin, hidden in a secret folder on my tablet that (hopefully) neither he nor Mabh can access and – just in case – I've encrypted this report as well.

I've spent the last three days poring over the report, looking for hints and answers.

And I've found more questions than anything.

Was Anupet the only one who could create Menacing Hobs or merely the first? If the former, does that mean we're rid of them forever? If the latter, who else is taking the dead of Faerie and corrupting them in such a foul, anathematic way?

Light enquiries through Taliesin's network of informants and covert agents in the Northern Realms of Faerie confirm two attacks in Meidhmæris in the waning days of December; Meidhmæris, where the Eye of Ma'at had been before winding up in Carterburg with a runaway faerie. That part of her path checks out. But … did Anupet actually *escape* Her or was she merely let loose in some gross ploy and newest move in the Mad Queene's long-game of Faerie Senet between the Courts?

How did Blodeuwedd realize or recognize Anupet – was it a guess or was it something more? And what did she mean by calling him "Prince Sorrow" and "Sorrow Son of Grief" – did she recognize something in him?

On top of that, the files confirmed >everything< that Nomios and Blodeuwedd told us the other night – and more. Vague hints and attestations of double-dealings and clandestine alliances between mortal and Fae, between Selighe and Unselighe have left me almost queasy. I've been antsy and (if I'm honest, rather pissed off) unable to focus on much of anything as questions keep racing through my brain – questions that I need answered.

Curiosity is always going to be my downfall, isn't it?

END FILE

·············

"Oy Orielle – salut Sara – would it be possible to coffee?"

The rich scent practically hugs me as the bartenders laugh and Sara places a large, steaming mug in front of me before turning back to the usual patrons.

I've found myself again at a crossroads – when the mysterious and muddling get too much and I don't dare to ruminate further in my halls of the Hollow Hill or sharing my worries with Tam (who's on another 'Date Night In' with Simon), I've begun taking myself to *The* (literal) *Crossroads* and its enigmatic proprietrix.

Sensible? Not so much. But altogether enlightening regardless.

"Did you see the size of his bulge? I couldn't tell if that was a wallet shoved down the front of his pants or heaven," a handsome brunet beside me leans against the bar, his shirt riding up to expose tanned skin and a whorling green tattoo above his waistband. "Either way … I won't be home tonight so don't stay up."

Laughing and depositing a wad of bills for his tab, he turns towards the tall, blue-tinted Fae at the top of the steps and winks at his roommate before leaving; all eagerness and hormones.

Admittedly, the faerie – either a Nekk or Corbie by his imposing height and coloring – does seem to possess impressive *endowments* … but, whether that's Glamour or nature, the mortal can learn for himself.

(Okay, sometimes it's merely entertaining.)

Behind the bar, and a moment free from her customers, I try not to pry as Orielle steals a quick kiss from Faun; one of the most recent additions to The Material Girls – Tori's a drag king who manages to blend posh glamor with an otherworldly satyr aesthetic. They're cute together and, again, I feel that old twinge of 'why not me?' before wiping it away with a swallow of coffee.

Smiling, I take the mug and make my way towards the back offices; threading my way through diners and die-hard dancers, tapping the mental connections I have with the surveillance Glamours and cantrips we've placed around the bar and accessing the ones Nomer has given Tam and me leave to.

In my mind's eye I flit through the different feeds; swift flowing vignettes of friends dancing, couples snogging, Go-Go boys getting tips, performers- wait. Back to that furtive pair jaggedly angling for the shadows – they could be up to something?

Focusing, I mentally enlarge the image and am greeted with the sight of Tam and Simon leaning against the old brick wall near the club's southwest corner; their hands going …

I break off and laugh, trying not to simultaneously feel like some sort of old prude and peeping tom as I focus back on why I came.

So many of the questions that dance behind my eyes all seem to lead back to the complex and discordant knowledge of the Stuarts and their role in Carterburg and Faerie's entwined history. Frustration hammers beside curiosity and, right now, the only Faerie who seems capable of leading me along this trail is …

"Blodeuwedd? Are you free?" I rap on the sturdy office door, my knuckles loud against it. "It's Cir-"

I don't even finish my name before the door has swung open and I'm greeted by Blodeuwedd at his desk, dinner laid out, with Johann – the erstwhile Lady Ophelia – and Nomios as well. No extravagant or artsy Glamours or make-up adorn them as the three sit in convivial company, eating their supper.

"I'm sorry – I can come back later if you'd like; I didn't mean to interrupt," I turn to leave.

"Please, Enchantress," Blodeuwedd smiles – over what smells delightfully like roast duck in garlic and shallots – and beckons me to join them. Nomios already had a spare chair pulled aside for me, "Feel free to tuck in. There's duck, asparagus, spanakopita, and – just for you – fresh-made butterfly pastries in anticipation."

The raised brow and just-shy-of-smug pitch on his lip makes me wonder whether they had a wager going on 'when' and 'whether' I'd put in an appearance. For a moment, my mood darkens and my hackles threaten to rise at this presumption, but, seeing their open faces, I swallow my own sharp reaction and take my seat before raising my coffee in salute. Despite it, I can feel a smile tugging at my lips and let its humor color my tone instead.

"Who won the bet?"

All three laugh loud, honest peels and I can feel the tenseness melting from my shoulders.

Johann's body-shaking laugh manages to jostle a lanky black and white cat on his lap who looks up with wide green-gold eyes and more patience than I've ever felt in my long life. It doesn't take Faerie sight to see that this isn't a mortal housepet – the lingering scent of stardust and twilight alone attest to that; but it's the small, half-grown wings wrapped about his torso that shout the Sidhe Cat's nature to all.

"I did – we all knew you'd show, but," Blodeuwedd tipped his glass towards the Puca, "Nomios was convinced you'd arrive yesterday and Johann was sure you'd come straight here from the field the other day; me? I guessed you needed longer to … ruminate."

And it's true, I did.

Nodding a wry smile, I nibble at the asparagus and duck waiting for the right moment to approach the tangle of my thoughts.

"Thank you, Circe," Johann's bright blue eyes hold me, warm and approachable, as he absently pets the cat; scritching behind its ear. "For sending us to help the Mourae; I know these two already have, but … I'd be a giant asshat if I didn't add my own thanks. *Our* thanks, right Merlin?"

Running his index finger beneath the cat's chin, a deep purr envelopes the room and shimmering the air with hints of springtime dusk.

"The Lady Euphrosyne saw this little runt and knew he'd have a better chance of a happy life (filled with snacks and treats) with someone to cater to his every whim instead of 'the wilds' of their valley – don't I, behbeh?"

The self-satisfied smile and continued purring confirm Merlin's own opinion on the subject.

A cat person: I knew I liked the queen.

"I'm glad that it all worked out," I start, but the tangle of nerves and questions gets the best of me and I don't finish the thought. Setting down my fork and pulling the coffee close to my chest I stare at the three.

"But, did it though?"

"Whatever do you mean, Enchantress?" While still warm, the familiarity in Blodeuwedd's voice has leeched off, replaced by almost-formal curtness.

"Those reports that Ciaran compiled told a lot more about recent events than I think I was ready for," I admit – the frustration and confusion coloring my voice.

"I was assuming they might," leaning back, Blodeuwedd dabs at his lips – the color in his mercurial eyes settling to a polished pewter – and focuses on me.

"How can I clear things up for you? What questions are within my power to answer you, O' Storied Agent of Queene and Country? What mysteries might I solve?"

His tone is half sing-song … and, as well as we're getting along I can't help but wonder if he's mocking me.

Silently, Nomios and Johann lean back from their dinner plates and watch.

"First, Anupet – how did you know? And, second, why did she call you 'Prince Sorrow'?"

"I didn't quite, I mostly guessed – truth be told. The same passage describing the Eye of Ma'at I showed you mentioned, about halfway down the page, its guardians: the sisters Anupet and Imentet; and since the boggle bore more of a canine appearance than avian …" Blodeuwedd spreads his hands, elegant rings glinting in the office's light. "As for

'Prince Sorrow'? I can't quite say for certain – perhaps she mistook me for another?"

My eyebrow is somewhere near my hairline: Blodeuwedd can't think this little of me.

"Or perhaps," he edges, choosing his words carefully. "She thought to impugn me as a Faerie Monarch. Or, the most likely, was mocking me as a 'notorious' drag queen and effete."

"I'll confess, I'd thought much the same," I meet him halfway at this explanation, but, still, it niggles at me – the uncertainty and his deflection; and so I file it away. "Although, it's curious how she acted as if she knew you, despite protestations."

"Madness, Enchantress, seldom has logical explanations; although, perhaps, if she served Angroboda in Her Court, she knew of the Mad Queene's distaste for me and *The Crossroads*."

I nod; it's a valid explanation even if it's utter bollocks.

One more mystery to add to the pile, methinks.

"And while I'm at it," I smile, my face stiff with uncertainty. "The third: Marleigh Lynn Stuart-Miller and the Bluebeard Gronw?"

The sigh from Blodeuwedd and arch look from Nomios confirm my worry that this was both a sore subject and one long-anticipated.

"I guessed as much and wondered when the Stuart connection would lead back to them," Blodeuwedd's voice is weary but, there is no animosity to it nor does is sound like danger couched in veiled hints. Regardless of a faerie's inability to outright lie, the hesitation and trepidation tell me that this will be the truth as >he< sees it.

"Wine?"

Pouring himself another glass of honey-golden wine, he passes another to me before pouring it out for Nomios and Johann.

"While she might have been kind to her 'staff' at home, Ms. Stuart was a ruthless and single-minded mortal – as much as her great, great grandmother, that thrice-damned harridan the fair Lucy's mother; if not moreso."

I barely stifle my incredulous gasp and snort – nothing, and I mean *nothing*, from the interviews with coworkers or my continued interactions with *On a Whim*'s faerie staff, have indicated anything of the sort.

"Her work as a Law Clerk and Title Examiner gave her access to Carterburg's entire Court Offices and her greed saw her manipulating land deeds, property titles, and historical edicts all for personal gain. You saw, just as I did, reading the old files how historical discrepancies suddenly began playing a bigger part in the last five years; in fact, ever since she joined Dunham, Perham and Yeates and the cases she was associated with."

I scoff at this, the disbelief plainly writ on my face, but nod.

"Regardless of what or how she behaved at home towards powerless underlings – and for all I know, or care, she genuinely loved them; who could say or gainsay? What I *do* know is that about six years ago she began working with 'Garner' whom we all know better as Gronw Pebyr. What we *both* may not know is that he was an envoy from Angroboda; one of her more disreputable agents, often used to torture and kill pronounced 'enemies of the crown' – much in the same way her bloody-handed son, Nemedh, has; a task he relished as you may recall."

Blodeuwedd's pointed tone drops me back into the dank and bloodied pocket room I found Marleigh's body in –

the musky darkness filled with menacing echoes and stifled screams and sobs – and it's several heartbeats (and a buttery pastry) before I regain my composure.

Coolly watching, Blodeuwedd sips at the wine – all planned composure.

Beneath my still smile, I'm trying not to clench my jaw.

"And from the vast array of monsters in Her Court, Gronw was one of the best suited to a more *discreet* mortal seeming here in-town, masquerading as a 'normal gentleman' of merit and company – the only telltale of his true nature, his affection for that damnable beard. From what he let slip to bartenders and performers in his many visits – myself included, he was tasked with 'securing' land and power; entangling anyone who could help him – and, by inference, *Her* – with Unselighe interests."

I'd have to be the most oblivious cat in creation to miss that he's choosing his words carefully and, despite the near-extemporaneous delivery, this is a speech he's rehearsed. From the controlled conversational tone to the acidic digs and reminders and the almost casual cadence as he admits his own perfidy, it's patently obvious that he's prepared this.

Blodeuwedd's a consummate performer doing his best to protect himself and/or his friends from being implicated too deeply in Gronw's actions.

Why must he make this so complicated?

"It's not easy to prove by mortal laws, but his work with Nnugia can be traced to several bodies – mortal *and* faerie – dumped in alleyways over the last few years, each one mangled almost beyond recognition." Nomios' concern cuts through the performance – and I can feel my mood softening.

Nodding, Blodeuwedd continues, "Would it surprise you to learn that Ms. Stuart helped him secure properties under various shell companies and shadowed names? Each one connected back to Angroboda and the Unselighe Court? Outside of the simple breach of formal agreements between the Courts, their tacit agreements concerning Carterburg and mortal lands, can you guess the 'why' of where she would?"

My mind reels at this tack, but not so much that I can't recall several of the deeds he's mentioned or overlaying their property lines across my mental map of Carterburg, Stefford, and Spotswood.

I gasp in shock when I realize that at least two of them are sites where we've found Sidhe Rings.

"Bluddy Hels," I bark. "She can't be?"

"She would and She is." Blodeuwedd's tone has slipped into bitter weariness as he sips at the wine, his hand resting on the teak box nearby. "Angroboda has been maneuvering for years now and after Her little display through Nnugia before Christmas – and their blatant interest in the potential power beneath *The Crossroads* – would you put any of it past Angroboda in the least?"

No.

I shake my head and sigh.

Despite his speech and its blatant purpose to quell my doubts, I can't help but want to take him – take them – at his word.

However, with Blodeuwedd's absolute determination to dance around it, there's a singular conclusion I'm reluctant to draw; there's still one question I have to know the answer to even if I don't want to.

It's been nipping at me ever since the other night, when he darkly referred to Lucy as "the aberration in that family; not the norm". And, perhaps, even longer – if the Fates be true; Tam's follow-up investigation while I was recovering from the fight with Gronw placed the beast often at *The Crossroads* and in its proprietrix' wake in the weeks leading up to Marleigh Lyn's disappearance and death. If I don't ask it, it will linger – hanging above everything like a damnable Sword of Damocles, ready to come down swinging at the worst possible time.

"So, you encouraged him to kill her?"

I don't think I've seen him actually surprised before.

"I … ", his silvery eyes glow for a moment before sensibility reigns in temper. "I *used* Gronw."

As he hesitates, closing his moon-cold eyes, I watch as he all-but wriggles in his seat choosing his next words carefully. For the first time tonight I see the 'real' Blodeuwedd beneath the control, the friend I >want< to trust.

Even if he's murdered an innocent (or not-so-innocent).

With a long sigh and sidelong glance at Nomios and Johann, he slugs back the rest of his wine.

"Did I encourage him to find out more on her actions and choices through sexual favors because I knew that that was the one-and-only way anyone aside from Angroboda Herself could attain any control over him? Did I encourage their liaisons because I knew the ill she did? Did I set him up to be caught by you that night because I hated him for his own monstrous actions before and for what he and Ms. Stuart were doing? Did I take out my intense, unyielding, and undying hatred of the Unselighe Queene and Court on him, Her instrument? For my own relief at his just punishment for what he'd done to her and countless other mortals and faeries across the realms?"

Did he?

"Did you?"

Beneath the control in my voice, I taste copper – I think I've bitten my tongue. I flinch, remembering the acrid taste of his blood as we struggled; both of us shifting forms as we fought, dragon and troll, bleeding, biting and clawing … until I'd killed him and lain his corpse at my Queene's slippered feet.

"Yes."

There's no anger in his voice; only clear, cold certainty.

"Do I regret Ms. Stuart's death? She and her family have done many, many, wrongs to Faeriekind over the last 150 years – how much blood was on her family's hands? How much is on her own?"

Standing, he's pushed himself away from the desk as he starts to pace around his chair. "Circe, you sat here in this office and heard what they did, how many innocent faeries the Stuarts themselves assured an early grave – you saw how they shied in Ofn Mynydd when they awoke. You heard how many they condemned to miserable lives barely eking out enough to sustain them in inhumane conditions and, when they could, they bullied and shorted them."

His temper, like his eyes, is mercurial and flashing.

Raw and volatile like I've not seen before.

"Through her own conscious choices she had a relationship with a serial killer/possible mass-murderer and – knowingly or otherwise – helped a Court of murderers, nightmares, blood-drinkers, and living death attain >*verifiably LEGAL*< footholds here in lands supposedly safe from them."

Throwing himself back into the chair, his outburst finished, Blodeuwedd's tone's changed; softening but still accusatory. And far from forgiving.

"How many Menacing Hob or bloodied monster attacks on innocent mortals can you trace back to properties Ms. Stuart helped deed to the Unselighe Court? How many monsters have you had to kill because of her?"

"What was done in the heat of the moment – in self-defense or in defense of others is one thing, but …" I stammer.

"None of us have hands clean of death or pain," Phuc's eyes are half-lidded as he stares at his own, neatly-trimmed nails; his voice haunted. "We all have to answer for that in the end."

I return to the original point, flustered by this tack and the dark thoughts it promises to dredge up, "The more you say, the less I know for certain, *your Majesty*. But, what I do know is that whether you meant it or not, your actions condemned her to death."

Despite myself I can't excise the memory of her mutilated body hanging from chains and painted in her own blood. In the back of my mind I note that the room feels warmer; in the reflection on a glass-fronted cabinet I can see a thin halo of amber sparks crackling amidst my hair, my own temper getting the best of me.

"You may as well have chained her up yourself; you damned her to a gruesome and malicious death without the benefit of trial. An excruciating end, mind you, you've done your damnedest to keep those you profess to care about from enduring." I slam my hand on the desk, "You played the part of judge, jury, and executioner-by-proxy."

"I am a queen of Faerie – monarchs aren't always afforded otherwise."

"That's fuckall, and you know it." I'm shouting and I can't help it; this whole theatrical dance of words has gone on too damn long. "Making that deliberate, cold and inhumane choice – how does that make you any better than them? Than *Her*?"

Mouthing a silent 'Oh', I watch as he draws his hand to his mouth; clenching his pale knuckles between teeth in puzzlement, thoroughly chastised by this realization; violent shimmers of starlight fading to dusk around us.

Beside me, Nomios' golden eyes well in concern as he reaches across to hold Blodeuwedd's other hand, whispering comforting words I do my best not to hear and rescind the Glamour about me. Running my hands through my hair I smell faint whiffs of candle flame and singed fur, the lingering taste of ancient rhymes sung on the bright ocean breeze is in the air; a hymn to father Helios.

I grimace in half-apology to Johann who weakly smiles, brushing away my concerns from a safe distance. "Don't worry – just give him a moment," he stage-whispers, hugging

Merlin to his breast. I hadn't meant to scare them, but this had to be sussed out.

Despite our friendship's newness, it pains me to see Blodeuwedd dropped into such total confusion and uncertainty; the mask of aloof enigmatic Fae stripped bare.

I feel awful, but I needed to do it; it needed to happen.

I can only guess what pain and trauma drove him to such rigidity. So much of what and who he is – as Blodeuwedd the Miss Nomer, as the Queen of Blood and Glitter – is crafted by adamantine control. Control of himself, of his emotions and his actions; of the planned long-term outcome of choices he makes. Of the consequences for those choices.

But this?

Right here, right now?

He can only control one thing: himself.

I hope that he's the Faerie beneath the Glamours and gowns that I've come to respect because his choice will determine how everything goes forward between us – between the Selighe Court and the Court of Blood and Glitter.

"Do I regret her death?" his voice is a scant echo of the force from a moment ago. "Once I would have answered you unflinchingly that for what she and hers did she deserved it all – and perhaps more."

Slowly, smiling weakly, the petal-marks along his cheeks gleaming like dark tears in the lamp light, he turns back to me, "Now? I honestly don't know. But I do regret her pain and the pain her loss has wrought; I sorrow that my direct actions have caused this pain."

"Thank you; that you don't know – that you regret the pain – gives me hope," I stand, still holding the coffee and smile. "It means more than you can guess." While several questions still linger, and a vague uncertainty hovers behind my eyes, I think that I'm willing to overlook them for now – our friendship is both a professional boon and a balance that I hadn't realized I was missing.

"I'm glad, Enchantress – Circe." The use of my real name is tentative on his lips and I smile in encouragement. "I'm sure that you know all too well what it's like for memories to eat away at you – memories of regret, remorse, loss, and anger." His voice is weary and thick like molasses, "Their pain is like salt on an open wound; your inability to avenge yourself upon those who hurt you and those you care for haunting you every night when you close your eyes."

"Take it from someone who knows, Blodeuwedd, vengeance isn't the same as justice; it's a twisted ouroboros feeding on itself in an endless cycle until you become that which you hate."

From across the desk I watch as his hoary eyes swiftly glow anew, like twin fiery moons of anguish and adamant – the room nearly quakes in opalescent rainbows beneath his fervor; the meekness of a moment before all-but forgotten in his confident vehemence.

"I promise you, Enchantress, I shall **NEVER** be like them - like *Her* – I would sooner die."

The sheer magnitude of power he's laced into those words of command and binding rattles me to my roots – beside him Johann flinches and Nomios closes his eyes (in grief?) – and I almost drop my coffee in surprise. Despite my misgivings and uncertainties, if there's any one thing that I can trust beyond a shadow of a doubt about Blodeuwedd, it's his hatred of Angroboda and Her Court – I have faith that he will fight them with everything he has.

Stray wisps and crackles of silvery, rainbow'd magic and Glamour dance like fireflies and falling ash throughout the office in its aftermath.

Coming around the desk, I tentatively pick up his hand and hold his shimmering eyes. "Anupet broke because she was alone in her grief and all-consuming need for vengeance, *we* don't have to be. *You* don't have to be, Blodeuwedd. You have friends," I nod towards the pair whose worried glances had almost left me in reproach. "You have a Court and you have people to protect."

"Thank you, Circe. I do, indeed, have a Court and *friends* to protect."

I can't help but feel a moment of pleasure at his emphasis on 'friends' as he stands, smiling at me; his hands on Nomios' and Johann's shoulders.

"I'm just glad that we can count one another in that category, Blodeuwedd," I add, unlooked for relief flooding me; my voice awkward and tentative, but encouraged. I'm still uncertain how things may play out, going forward, but, I'm hopeful.

"Ah, fair Enchantress, do not reprehend, if you pardon I shall mend," bowing and winking, Blodeuwedd doffs a Glamoured Venetian mask of onyx ivy and silvery horn that hadn't been there a moment before.

"Give me your hands, if we be friends, and Robin –
well, Nomer – shall restore amends."

I don't think I've gladly snorted, nearly choking on
coffee, laughing so hard in ages. And it's a wonderful feeling.

EPILOGUE

... deep within Faerie

The witch's adept sat cross-legged, his cloak an inky abyss lost amidst the gloom, and watched a pair of handsome partygoers in ruddy golden garb wend their way through an alley in the seediest part of town. Unseen, he sighed out at the night.

He could wait.

Meidhmæris stood in sullen shadow beneath the forbidding peaks of the Jókkgrímnarr Mountains; a dark gem of rough edges and baroque frailty garbed in ancient wood, tarnished brass and chipped marble.

Tonight, as was often the case, the city folded in on itself against the foetid chill that permeated its winding streets; doors were locked and windows shuttered. The icy waters of Evendim barely rippled beneath the green vapors and sulfurous flames of blue and yellow that flickered up from the depths and danced, like ghosts, down the labyrinthine corridors and alleyways that made up the quayside neighborhoods; casting skittering and disquieting shadows against wall and stone.

They said, the city's fathers and forefathers, that the city was haunted by the decaying spirits of its choices; its mistakes were the ghostly memories that troubled it on dark, cold nights.

Away in the south they said that Meidhmæris was cursed; a city of the dead and damned – tarted up in its forgotten funerary finery in its best efforts to hide the truth from itself.

Hope, they said, bubbled like a dying man's breath in the city; where rejected courtiers and duelists sought tricks and traps to find themselves back into Her Dark graces ... while giving themselves over to the darkest pleasures of blood and sex in the city's seedier corners.

The dry scholars of prestigious schools and learned libraries across Faerie were of the opinion that the city lay in an ancient caldera whose sulfur (and other noxious fumes) interacted most strangely (yet explicably) with the salt-waters of Evendim on chill nights. And, when prodded, they added in hushed tones that many of the city's troubles stemmed more from the urban mismanagement of drunkards and hedonists than from the fall of its once-proud ruler, the Queene's Champion.

Whatever the truth, the city was stricken – with the rescinding of the Queene of Night's approval centuries ago – and its name unspoken by none in the upper echelons of the Unselighe Court. Instead, brigands, thieves, whores, witches, the Disavowed – Fae who could not bring themselves to abandon the Unselighe territories, but fallen out of favor with Her Dark Majesty – and those who wished to hide from Her sight called it home.

Pulling back his hood, the witch's adept stared at the heavens and searched for unasked answers among the constellations.

A shooting star illuminated him in its rutting path between heaven and earth; catching his eyes (of a color he always likened to a Selkie's kiss) and flattering his sharp nose and supple cheek above surprisingly full lips that curved downwards in an almost perpetual frown. Unruly waves of bark-black hair tumbled to his shoulders while thin, sharp horns of a grey-gold darker than his cool skin curved backwards and met the bright gold of his earrings; jewelry that mirrored the bracelets and numerous rings – each etched with sigils and runes of power and warding – he always wore as he absentmindedly drummed his fingers along the stone of the rooftop.

The pale silver horn of Faerie's grandest moon danced high in the sky as the adept watched the pair drunkenly stagger further into the maze, still searching for their goal. He cocked his brow as it hovered, seemingly over his shoulder like a great pet; its pale beauty illuminating the dilapidated form of the Temple at the acropolis – long plundered and left to rot. Slowly, its smaller lunar brethren swayed in succession; their bulbous shapes silhouetting the mountains that ringed the city's edge like jagged teeth.

And he waited.

Rumors flew about the city these days, like malformed ravens, that the Queene's dead heart might have begun a change; that Her temper towards the Dispossessed of Meidhmæris could be … assuaged.

A Champion was needed, they said.

A fighter who – should things turn sour with Queene Mabh and the Selighe Court or, more likely, Queene Angroboda decided to expand Her reign within Faerie – would stand for them all. Who would stand at Her side – loyal, powerful, unwavering and, beyond all, deadly.

He would have the Queene's ear, they said.

Hope and fear entwined themselves throughout the city at the thought.

Even now, in those Duelist Clubs – like the one he hoped to track tonight – courtiers and the fat-pursed gentry wagered on fighters. Procurers brought Fae from across the vast stretches of the Northern Realms; gnome, Ettin, troll, Jotunn, Dókkalfar, and a dozen other breeds and class of Fae fought and died in gross displays of machismo. Should She choose Meidhmæris' champion in the contest, perhaps (they hoped) She would forgive them and return the city to its proper place as Her crown jewel. After all, they reasoned, it'd been centuries since She'd leveled the fortress of Gnaffættr Keep, high above the city, in Her displeasure.

Surely, by now, with the right Champion, Her opinion would soften.

He and others bit their tongues at this for had not Her anger always seemed implacable, despite the hopeful rumors that kept so many abuzz as of late.

The witch's adept had little interest in the fights' eventual outcome, he was sure She would still snub their city regardless and, if truth-be-told, he hoped for it; Her attention was dangerous beyond words and he enjoyed the anonymity forgotten Meidhmæris afforded.

He sought the Duelists not for their hope (what could it do for him – could it feed him? Clothe him? Protect him from his enemies or avenge his pain upon them? Hope was empty as air to him), but for their wallets and their well-lined costuming. Although rent on the hovel of an apartment he called home was negligible, his teacher – the disgraced witch, Mother Ænthannia – enjoyed the occasional bauble or bribe for lesson and company.

And, most of all, he sought them for the persistent rumor that the city's champion might be a particular Dókkalfar; a tall, well-built faerie whose kisses had tasted like Elfwine and whose touch had left the adept drunk on love … before dashing his heart and hopes when the bastard disappeared without a word years before.

A tang of ozone and a burst of neon green down a side-street told him that the pair had found their way into the hidden club. Pulling his hood back up, he concentrated, muttering words of command and seeming, and thrilled at the silken kiss of a courtier's Glamour enveloping him from head to toe.

If she met him tonight, even his own mother wouldn't recognize him.

That thought brought a rare smile to the adept's lips.

He planned to find Svipdagr and, whether by blade or by kiss, to crack his heart in turn if he could. Or break his bones if he must. He would have his revenge and no one, not even the Mad Queene Herself, would get in his way.

TO BE CONTINUED in

A THRONE OF ILL-MADE WILL

the fourth volume in
A Queen of Blood and Glitter

PRONOUNCIATION GUIDE

(unless otherwise noted, the languages are the ancient forms not their modern counterparts – Egyptian, Attic Greek, etc)

- **Addanc / Afanc** (ahh-dTHANK / ahh-VANK) Welsh: a lake monster that resembled the worst traits of dragon, crocodile, and beaver; it dwelled near Llyn Afanc (the lake named after it) devouring maiden and hero (was invisible when it chose) and was eventually slain by Peredur with aid from the Glain Nadir, a giant seeing stone that broke through its spells

- **Ahew** (EH-hoo) "Grief" Egyptian

- **Aneirin** (ah-NEE-rin) Welsh: one of the five greatest bards of the Isle of Britain, served notable rulers Urien and

Owain in the late 6th century CE before the fall of the Brythonic kingdoms to the Anglo-Saxons and wrote the epic Y Gododdin after the Battle of Catraeth; serves Taliesin as his right hand in spycraft and bardcraft within Faerie and The Hollow Hill for the last 1400 years

- **A'nen** (ah-NEN) "Bring Back" Egyptian
- **Angroboda** (AHN-grow-boe-duh) "She Who Brings Grief" Norse; Queene of the Unselighe Court, mother to Nemedh and Blodeuwedd (and many others); she is incredibly dangerous – a Jotunn Frost Fae many millennia old, she began as one of the many wives of the Unselighe King and either advanced past or slew his other wives; called also The Mad Queene, The Queene of Night, The Unselighe Queene, The Dark Queene, etc
- **Ankh udja seneb** (AHnK oodj-uh SENN-eb) "Life, strength, health" Egyptian, a prayer and, in Anupet's use, a powerful command in magic
- **Anupet** (AH-noo-pet) "Lady of Decay" [*conjectural*] Egyptian; the counterpart to Anubis, Lord of the Dead and Decay, the deity especially associated with the afterlife (called the Duat); with her sister, Imentet, they helped mortals within their great temple complex (near The

Valley of The Kings in modern Egypt) through the power of the gem, The Eye of Ma'at; the temple was ransacked by Angroboda and Her forces near the end of The Great War where the sisters were taken captive, tortured, and used over the millennia; Anupet, by accident, became Angroboda's tool in creating Menacing Hobs and was broken by grief and loss

- **Anubis** (AH-noo-biss) "Lord of Decay" [*conjectural*] Egyptian; god of the dead and the afterlife (Duat) and husband to Anupet; with much of his family, during The Great War, he slipped between the cracks to escape – choosing neither to aid the Selighe nor the Unselighe Courts, unfortunately his wife and sister-in-law were left behind

- **Aw ibetj / ibek** (AWW ibetJ / ibeK) "May your heart rejoice" (ibetj is fem, ibek is masc) Egyptian

- **bàsachadh mu thràth** (BAY-sawkkaTH moo thAYth) "(Oh just) die already" Scots Gaelic

- **Ben Beirdd** (BEN beirdTH) "Chief of Bards" Welsh, epithet of Taliesin

- **Blodeuwedd** (BLOW-dew-wedTH) "Flower Face" Welsh 1) magically created wife of Lleu Llaw Gyffes in the Welsh mythic cycle

2) chosen name of the son of Angroboda, also known as the Miss Nomer, a moon-cold faerie who claimed a crown as The Queen of Blood and Glitter – chosen as the tear-scarred marks on his cheeks resemble petal marks, despite being originally a faerie of Angroboda's Northern Realms

- **Blüdmoss** (blood moss) a type of moss that has a coagulant property in its roots and fibrous material, found in the lee of Standing Stones within Sidhe Rings

- **Ciaran** (KEER-uhn) also named Chios Ran (KEE-yohs RANN) a Lares, household faerie spirit who has served Mabh for millennia, protecting the amount of/veracity of mortal reckonings of Faerie history

- **Circe** (SEER-SEE, properly KEER-KEE) "The Cycle" Greek (from Kirkoo "encircled in magic") – daughter of Helios, demigoddess, former queen of Colchis and Aeaea, sister of Pasiphe and Aeetes, ex-love of Odysseus and cousin to High Queene Mabh; a Sidhe Cat, shapeshifter extraordinaire, Chief Investigator for HRH and member of the Queene's Privy Council (*prefers the Anglicized pronunciation of her name*)

- **Cybele** (KIH-bell-hey) Phrygian (?) possibly "Mountain Mother"; the first and eldest of all Fae and the cult/temples to her are the only 'true' organized religion across their cultures (found in regions under Angroboda just as easily as Mabh or even small cave-temples on Midgard)

- **Dókkalfar** (DOHKK-ahll-farr) "Dark Elves" a type of Fae, generally possessing dark grey-gold skin and bright gold eyes with shimmering dark blonde or black hair

- **Élivágor** (EHLLi-VAH-gorr) "Icy Waves" Norse; the great city of tall spires, many temples, and beautiful architecture – in bright, icy marble and gilt – that replaced Meidhmæris as the crown jewel of Angroboda's realm; many preeminent libraries, including The Dókkalfar Library, and schools ring the city; it sits at the brunt of the Nidavellir plains with the great palace of Niffelheim along the seaside edge of the city and, away southeast, the great Ironwood

- **Euphrosyne** (YOU-froz-in-ay) "Joy/Merriment" Greek; one of the three Graces / Charites and guardian of the Baetylus and the Mourae (the cat-owl soul-ferriers for Cybele); grandmother of Nomios Phuc

- **Evendim Lake** (EE-ven-dim) Lake fed by the great river Vulga (mirrors the same river on earth) as it flows from the

Jókkgrímnarr Mountains to the great sea; the city of Meidhmæris sits along it (many, many miles southwest is the great city of Élivágor)

- **Feck** (FEKK) "fuck" Gaelic variant
- **Glain Neidr** (GLAYn neyh-Dhur) Welsh; the Welsh name for hag stones/adder stones/witch stones – stones with naturally occurring circular openings (thought to be produced by serpent venom) that can see through Glamours – the great Glain Nadir, granite and roughly a meter in size, was found by Peredur during his battle with the Addanc and helped him break through its invisibility Glamour
- **Glamour** (GLAM-ohr) the name for the all-purpose magic of seeming and un-seeming that most Fae can be trained to use – from simple beauty visual to more substantial shapeshifting or teleportation; a seeing stone's natural magic can interrupt it or even, when joined by antagonistic magic, be used to break it
- **Gnaffættr Keep** (gNAV-aedr) "Supernatural Tower" (Norse) the grand tower and fortress at the height of Meidhmæris where Angroboda's chosen, the Queene's Champion, lived until She sent Her agents to kill him and

his retainers; afterwards, She destroyed most of the Keep and turned Her back on Meidhmæris

- **Haty-ek em mi kha** (hahTEE-eck emm meek kHA) "Your mind is like an empty room" Egyptian, classic insult
- **Hat-ib** (HOTT-eeb) "Sadness" Egyptian
- **Hecate** (he-KAHH-tay) Pre-Greek origins name (possibly hqt [heKAHt], Egyptian for "magic"); the Greek goddess of witchcraft, magic, and crossroads – often depicted as a triple/triptych goddess of three faces
- **Iad** (EE-ahd) "they" Scots Gaelic
- **Ianew** (EE-yah-NOO) "Sorrow" Egyptian
- **Ianew Sen'Ahew** (EE-yah-NOO SENyah-HOO) "Sorrow Son of Grief" Egyptian; the name Anupet calls Blodeuwedd [*as Angroboda's name means "She Who Brings Grief" it cannot be coincidence that she calls him that – surely recognizing him, whether he realizes that or not …*]
- Ibetj teftef haty-ek mehy (ibetJ TEF-teff HOT-ee-ekk meh-HE) "Your heart is disturbed and your senses scattered" Egyptian curse
- **Imentet** (IH-men-tet) "She of the West" Egyptian, Kite/Falcon headed goddess of the Western Lands (of

funerary lands), guardian of the Mansions of the Dead and sister to Anupet

- **The Iárnvidir** (YARN-vidd-eer) "The Ironwood" Norse; the great, dark forest in the Northern Realms of Faerie which stretched from the Nidavellir plains northwards to the Jókkgrímnarr Mountains and away east and south – home to monsters and many malicious Fae, including The Iron Witch (formerly Angroboda, currently Her daughter Ceinwyn)

- **Iusaaset** (YUh-sah-set) "She Who Grows as She Comes" Egyptian; goddess of creation and epithet of Cybele

- **Jókkgrímnarr** (YOHK-h-greem-nar) "Ice and Shadow" Norse; bastardization of Jokull ok grímna "Glacier Ice and Shadow" – the jagged and forbidding mountains that form the border between the "civilized" Northern Realms of Faerie and the Northern Wilds beyond of tundra, plain, and ice

- **Klepios** (klep-PEE-yohs) Greek, from 'Asklepios' (the Healer), one of Mabh's most capable and private doctors

- **Korvu** (KOR-VOO) the name for Raven faeries – specifically, those who serve royal houses as Guard; their lesser cousins, generally crow-based, are called Corbies

- **Kemet / Kemetan** (keh-MET / keh-MET-un) "The Black Land" the name for the fertile lands along the Nile, and subsequently, the original name for Egypt and Egyptians (which is a Greek word)

- **Lon Robbyn** (lonn ROB-binn) fallen courtier, resident of Meidhmæris, who took the chance to plunder The Temple (and many other nearby houses of Cybele worship) claiming it to be in the name of Angroboda, but keeping most of it for himself – he held the Eye of Ma'at before it was stolen

- **Ma'at** (MAh-AhT) "Balance" Egyptian; the goddess of balance and order

- **Mabh** (mahVV) from the proto-Irish 'Medua' "Intoxicating" and Irish Meadb "She Who Intoxicates"; the High Queene of Faerie, cousin to Circe and sister-in-law to Angroboda, wife to Taliesin

- **Meidhmæris** (mEYdTH-mehr-is) from meidmar "treasure" Norse; the former capital city of Angroboda's territories whose broken temples once housed the Eye of Ma'at

- **Mesneh** (mez-NEH) "turn backwards" Egyptian

- **Metrokoites** (meh-TROh-koy-tees) "shit" Greek

- **Nemedh Dolios** (NEMm-edTH) unknown, possibly related to Irish 'Nemed' / (DOhL-eeYOhS) "Tricky" Greek; The Phooka, favourite son of Angroboda – the only son of Angroboda and Dragul (Mabh's twin), trained by Loki and Niddhogge, Her ultimate weapon of chaos and murder and spy

- **Nidavellir** (nid-uh-VELL-LEER) "No Moon Plains" Norse; the great farmland and plains that makes up a substantial portion of the Northern Realms, bordered by mountain ranges and the Ironwood

- **Niddhogge** (NID-d-hOHg-ge) "Malice Striker" Norse; the great dragon who gnaws the roots of Yggdrasil, the World Tree – he trained both Angroboda and Her son Nemedh in the darkest and most-forgotten sorceries of Faerie or Man

- **Niffelheim** (NIhF-fell-hYM) "Home of Shadows and Mists" Norse; traditionally the palace/realm of the dead – the name Angroboda chose for Her palace in Élivágor

- **Nom de l'enquêteur** (nohmm dehl-enquAY-tour) "Investigator's Name" modern French; a play on nom de plume by Circe

- **Nomios Phuc** (NOH-me-yohs FOOK) "Shepherd" Greek "Pooka/Pooki/Puca" Celtic translation of the Norse Pooki;

son of Penelopeia and Pan, best friend to Blodeuwedd the Miss Nomer and Johann The Lady Ophelia

- **Ofn Mynydd** (awVn munn-OOdTH) "Pointe Dread" Welsh; literally the "mountain of dread", the grey-green bulwark fortress of Faerie along the Hedgeman's River between Summerduck and Goldvein communities in Fauquier County – hope to the Glain Nadir and the Peredurdr Order

- **Peredur** (pair-eh-DUR) Welsh; the hero who slew the Addanc with the aid of the Glain Nadir

- **Peredurdr** (pair-eh-DUR-der) "Of Peredur" Welsh; order of Fae priests who are tasked with guarding the Glain Nadir and using it to help foster the understanding of Faerie-upon-Earth [*and secretly use it to guard against Unselighe Glamours in the north and west of Carterburg*]

- **Phlegethon** (fleg-eth-awnn) "Flaming" Greek; one of the five rivers that flow through and around the Hellenistic and Roman underworld

- **Qeb-hut** (KEB-HOOT) "Cooling Water" Egyptian; Anubis and Anupet's serpent-headed daughter, the personification deity of the unguent waters used in embalming

- **Ra / Re** (Rah / Reh) "Sun disc" Egyptian; the personification deity of the noonday sun/high sun – the ultimate god within the Egyptian Pantheon for millennia (eventually merged with Amon/Ammun into Amon Ra)

- **Re'pat** (reh-PATt) "prince" Egyptian

- **Repyt** (REYP-et) Egyptian; Lioness-headed fertility goddess, daughter of Ra

- **Robhwyn London** (ROHbV-win Lun-dun) popular designer of jewelry in the late 19ᵗʰ century Washington DC area who set the Eye of Ma'at into The London Stuart Egg [*Circe suspects him to have a connection to Lon Robbyn, the unctuous Unselighe Fae – not only the similar name, but the connection via the Eye of Ma'at/London Stuart Egg*]

- **Seadh** (ShYADh) "yeah (affirmation)" Scots Gaelic

- **Selighe** (SEE-LEE) "kindly" Scots; the modern name for Mabh's Court, that prefers a more peaceful coexistence with mortals (eventually leaving for Faerie in the 6ᵗʰ – 9ᵗʰ centuries)

- **Senef** (SEN-eff) "blood" Egyptian

- **Sen / Senet** (SEN / SEN-ett) "Son"/ "Daughter" Egyptian [*the 'et' is the feminine ending*]

- **Senet** (seNET) "Passing" Egyptian; the Egyptian game of passing, maneuvers, and complicated long-form plotting (similar to chess) – whether Faeries invented it and gave it to the Egyptians or the Egyptians of the Pre-Dynastic era invented it and shared it with Mabh is argued on both sides of history [*despite similarity in pronunciation, the hieroglyphs differentiate the words senet (daughter) and Senet (the game)*]

- **Sewered pu djed en-ek** (se-WEhR-ed poo dJED enn-EhKK) "Just talking to/with you is exhausting" Egyptian curse

- **Sidhe** (sSHEEh) "The Mounds" Irish; the term for both the fairy mounds the Aos Sí/Aes Sidhe (AhSs sSHEEh) dwell in and the fairies themselves; a name for the Fair Folk in Irish and Scots mythology (and one of the many, many names Mabh endorses for the Fae); in modern Irish they are the Daoine Sidhe (ThEEneh sSHEEh)

- **Sprite fyre** – a form of Glamoured flame with its root spell akin to Will-o'-the-Wisps' and Pixies' own flame; it can be minor to light or dangerous like forest flame

- **Svipdagr** (sVIP-dahg-ur) "Sudden Day" Norse, a dangerous Dókkalfar – handsome and smart, reputed to battle for the right of Queene's Champion in Meidhmæris' Dueling Clubs (he is also the witch adept's ex-lover)

- **Svartalfar** (sVART-ahlFARr) "dark elves" Norse; a branch of Dókkalfar with their coloration inversed (darker skin, paler hair, all in grey-golds)

- **Tamlinn** (TAhM-LIN) Scots; a Dumnonii faerie (son of a faerie woman and mortal man) rescued by Mabh and brought to Court in the 6th century; a mis-remembering of his story became the Scots Border Ballad Tam Lin; he is the best friend and investigative partner to Circe and currently dating Simon Drake

- **Taliesin Kyanokhaitēs** (TAhL-yEeh-SIN kiy-YANn-OH-kHAY-TAYZ) Welsh and "Blue-Dark Haired" Greek; the Brythonic Welsh bard who happens to be Greek in origin – a Selkie Warchief and one of Mabh's generals and consorts during The Great War before becoming exclusive in the 11th century CE; chief of the Queene's Privy Council and Circe's boss

- **Unselighe** (UN-see-lee) "unkindly" Scots; the modern name for Dragul Kronos and Angroboda's Court of antagonistic faeries who see humanity as their prey

- **Wekha** (WEKK-hah) "fool" Egyptian

- **The War / The Great War** – The Trojan War, fought in the 12th Century BCE, ostensibly remembered for the Greek vs Trojans, but, the Selighe and Unselighe Courts fought around them as the 'Olympians' (that were split between the two sides); at the end of the war Dragul Kronos, King of the Unselighe, was locked away in Promethean exile forever and the Unselighe were greatly diminished
- **Wepset** (wep-SET) "She Who Burns" Egyptian, deity personification of the Uraeus (cobra-headed crown), called an Eye of Ra and sister to Sekhmet, the War Goddess
- **Wepwawet** (WEP-wah-wet) "Opener of the Ways" Egyptian; wolf-headed younger brother to Anubis; a war deity as well as the scout who leads the way through the Duat/afterlife
- **Wyrmroot** (WORM-root) a pleasant medicinal herb
- **Yaldi! Ullaich màthairfuckers** (yALLDEE yOOL-lake mah-thur-fuckers) "YEAH! Get ready motherfuckers" modern Scots Gaelic

I Keep Dancing
As My World Falls Down

– A playlist –

- **As The World Falls Down – David Bowie (Labyrinth soundtrack)**
- **Closure – Taylor Swift (Evermore)**
- **Dodgeball Daydream – (Were the World Mine soundtrack)**
- **Epiphany – Taylor Swift (Folklore)**
- **Evermore – Taylor Swift feat. Bon Iver (Evermore)**
- **Exile – Taylor Swift feat. Bon Iver (Folklore)**
- **Gold Rush – Taylor Swift (Evermore)**
- **Happiness – Taylor Swift (Evermore)**
- **Live to Tell – Madonna (Confessions on a Dance Floor LIVE)**
- **Mirrorball – Taylor Swift (Folklore)**
- **Mad Woman – Taylor Swift (Folklore)**

- Not Yet – Gladiator: More Music soundtrack
- Now We Are Free [Maximus Mix] – Gladiator: More Music soundtrack
- Shake It Out – Florence + The Machine (Ceremonials)
- Stud – Troye Sivan (In a Dream)
- Take Yourself Home – Troye Sivan (In a Dream)
- The Gladiator Waltz [Original Synth Demo Version] – Gladiator: More Music soundtrack
- Till the World Ends – Britney Spears (Femme Fatale)
- Warriors – AJ Michalka (She-Ra and the Princesses of Power soundtrack)
- Willow – Taylor Swift (Evermore)
- Wish That You Were Here – Florence + The Machine (Miss Peregrine's Home for Peculiar Children soundtrack)

CREDITS

Cover art:
"Anupet" by John M. Lee Jr.

Cover design:
John M. Lee Jr.

Interior art:
"Anupet" and "Menacing Hobs" by S. K. Wrenn

CLOSURE

[... aka an Afterword]

[25 years (and several wigs) later, this is still on-brand]

As I sit here writing this listening to Taylor Swift [*yes, I've finally become one of >those< gays who thinks Folklore and Evermore are a productivity gift from the writing gods*] I can't help but be blown away by the journey.

On the shelf beside me are a thicc AF novel built around several disparate and loosely connected geeky-folklore queer faerie adventures and its first companion novella ... and now? A third volume in the 'A Queen of Blood and Glitter' series has flown out into the world and I'm working on the (daunting) fourth installment: 'A Throne of Ill-Made Will'.

It's rather giddy and fizzy, when you stop to think about it.

Nine or so years ago I sat down and wrote the first words that described Miss Nomer – "an elaborately coiffed and be-decked drag queen with feathery horns entwined in her sky-high hair and impossibly sharp cheekbones who winked at Liam underneath glitter-stained false lashes" – and relegated her to the peripheral antagonist role of the Faerie Queen in my re-telling of Tam Lin [*Playing For Keeps, the first part of AQoBaG*].

But, she stayed in the back of my mind; biding her time. When she reappeared three-ish years later, while I was putting together 'A Case of Moon-Cold Silver for a horror/fantasy anthology, Nomer suddenly sported her signature petal marks, a 'real' name, and a rather nuanced and tragically dark back-story (as many intriguing, morally grey characters tend to).

From there, Blodeuwedd the Miss Nomer's appearances danced along the line between bitter decadence and fragile hope; between his hopeful (sometimes shitty, but always carefully chosen) actions in the here-and-now and the choices he made in his past – to embrace his pain and eschew joy in lieu of vengeance. By the end of AQoBaG Blodeuwedd's journey had (hopefully) shown his growth; from the heart-burnt young man who vowed vengeance no matter the cost [*see: Marleigh Lyn Stuart-Miller*] to someone who had finally pulled himself out of that yawning abyss of pain.

Admittedly, the love and trust of his two best friends – Nomios and Johann – could be the biggest attribution here.

Sidenote: I absolutely love writing about the deep (if occasionally fraught) friendship between these three. Three queer (gay and bi) men who are friends; too seldom do we get queer friendships in unabashedly queer literature – often sidelined as the best friend to the cishet white woman and her prop or relegated to the side-character sleeping his way through the town and offering witty one-liners [*don't get me wrong, the stereotype exists for a reason, but, it's not the only trope we exist as, pleaseandthankyou*]. Too often we perceive that in a story – especially a fantasy tale – that the only guarantee for happiness, for completeness, is romantic love. But, the friendships that bear us up; that support us in our darkest hours – our broken memories of ugly deeds and painful missteps – that offer us succor because they love us like that?

They are invaluable.

Of course, as Circe pointed out in the last chapter, whether her reasons were valid or no, there are still consequences for Blodeuwedd's choices. Yes, Circe understands [*insofar as Blodeuwedd has rationalized his choices to her – she still doesn't suspect his origins as Angroboda's runt though*], but, her job is still to investigate and lead criminals to justice; even if Blodeuwedd can't be charged due to the rules of Faerie Monarchic Law (he is a Queen of a Court), he isn't immune to the consequences of his actions. How will these

Impact their interactions and relationship going forward in 'A Throne of Ill-Made Will'? I can't wait.

Oh, and speaking of interactions:

What about that last-pages addition of Meidhmæris' own, the witch's adept and the hints of Svipdagr? Up until now, we've (somehow) managed to avoid much time in actual Faerie – focusing on Carterburg's complicated relationships – but the thought of bringing them and their lovers-to-enemies energy in from Faerie a tad earlier than planned was simply too wonderful to resist.

Forgive me?

-Benjamin Kissell
January 2021

ACKNOWLEDGMENTS

All of my thanks to my creative team (okay, that's mostly my friend Kay, my amazing husband and our cats, but still …) for the phenomenal work we've done putting this together.

When I sat down with the thought of putting together interim, shorter, stories between the first and second BIG novels it was really just to help me get past the giant impasse of a first draft of A Throne of Ill-Made Will and the burgeoning writing ennui of early Quarantining.

Those first sixty-odd pages?

Didn't gel.

Didn't feel right.

And, now? I realize why.

The story between Blodeuwedd's self-crowning in early December and where the second novel begins in spring had so many things that needed to be told and … honestly … flashbacks (while fun) were hampering what I needed to say.

Thankfully, my chief critical eye and biggest fan – my aforementioned husband – helped steer me right … whether it was listening to me vent or being the best of sounding boards. And, to be honest, so did Nomios – my dear, dear Puca. The revelation of the Stuart's secret history? Came out whole cloth in one sitting (revised and edited afterwards) as if Nomios himself were telling me the story.

Demanding it be told.

Thank you, John, for being the rudder and sail to my errant ship. For producing ANOTHER kick-ass cover painting and design – seriously, I'm luckier than I deserve to be. For helping me be unafraid of tropes and when their opposites are most-needed. For loving me (even and especially when I'm surly over my slow-moving 20ish year old laptop).

Thank you, also, to Kay for taking on the cold beauty and ugliness of my monsters.

Thank you to friends like Rosemary, Melissa(s as there are several), Rebekka, and Nate who support me, and to fans like Kevenn, Dawn and Joshy who never flag in their kind words and their fandom born of friendship; I wouldn't be writing these if not for y'all.

Thank you to my family – smaller this year with the loss of my surrogate father, Grandpa – for your love and for the art and literature you set in my heart at a tender age.

www.ingramcontent.com/pod-product-compliance
Lightning Source LLC
Chambersburg PA
CBHW072227170626
46813CB00003B/1114